*HONEYBEE RHYTHM*
A Mercy Mountain Novel

Copyright © 2021 by Becca Maxton

All rights reserved. Except for use in any review, the reproduction or utilization of this work in whole or in part in any form by any electronic, mechanical or other means, now known or hereinafter invented, including xerography, photocopying and recording, or in any information storage or retrieval system, is forbidden without the written permission of the publisher.

This is a work of fiction. Names, characters, places and incidents are either the product of the author's imagination or are used fictitiously, and any resemblance to actual persons, living or dead, business establishments, events or locales is entirely coincidental.

Printed in the USA.

Cover Design and Interior Format

# Honeybee
# RHYTHM

A
MERCY MOUNTAIN
NOVEL

# Becca Maxton

*Dedication*

*For J & M*

# Chapter 1

*Ashnee Valley, Colorado*

"LET ME GET THIS STRAIGHT. I walk all the way from here to there and when I get back you let me kiss you?" Jett Mannis pointed to the pine tree one hundred yards from where they stood on his family's property surrounding Mercy Mountain Lodge.

"By yourself," Delia added.

"By myself, the walking and the kissing," he said to his sister-in-law, Sofia's, best friend. "I ain't sharing you, woman."

Delia scoffed. "You're an idiot."

"Only for you, Honeybee."

"Well?" She lifted her bouquet of white and purple lilacs and sniffed. "Go on. I'll be waiting."

The way she smiled, just her blue eyes lifting to his, nose in the flowers, made him hard. He refrained from asking what he'd get if he walked a hundred yards there and back with a boner.

He set out, his cane leading the way, his left side bearing weight as he dragged his right side, stiff and weak. Hell, ever since his car accident less than a year ago, he'd been on the wagon, a beat up, tired, slow-recovering, and currently celibate wagon.

*This kiss better be worth the ache.* He grinned, knowing it would be.

He ambled forward, purposely lowering his shoulders to prevent a crick in his neck. A new cramp sparked his back every time he took a step. This was worse than physical therapy. He stopped and looked behind him, watching Delia swing the skirt of her cream-colored dress back and forth before pulling it up in front, gifting him with a flash of her tan, toned legs. Her laughter tickled the back of his neck as he turned again and headed for the tree.

Delia Kincaid. He'd kissed her months ago before she headed back to New York to her life as an actress. Besides his son, RJ, the kiss was a highlight of his early days of sobriety.

*Maybe she kissed me?*

After three months in the hospital following the crash, he left, unable to walk. He'd recuperated at the family ranch, equipped with a motorized scooter. He chuckled remembering how he'd let four-year-old, RJ, sit on his lap in those early days. At the time, Delia, cornered him to say a warm goodbye. He was in sorry shape back then.

*Maybe it was a pity kiss?*

His memory of the accident itself remained fuzzy even now. But in a small town like Ashnee

Valley, everyone knew the story. It wasn't beyond his family to retell it to any newcomers who hadn't heard it fifty times already.

"That night…" his brother-in-law, Leo, would say. "Jett had an argument with Jim and took off from their dad's ranch like a bat out of hell."

"He was scared," his older sister, Kai, might add. "He'd just found out he had a son he'd never known about."

"I'm the one Jett told first about RJ." Sofia, his brother's wife, would brag and smile modestly.

"Add in drunk," Jim always announced, "his go-to-state of being, and the fact he took the curve on Moonshine Ridge Road at a ridiculous speed."

Depending on who told the story, this was the point where a reenactment of his truck careening around a corner going anywhere from forty to a hundred miles per hour occurred.

"The perfect storm," his father, Ben, shook his head, "for driving through a fence and rolling onto the property of my neighbor's ranch."

The audience, regardless of who they were, always concluded the story the same way every single time. "You're lucky you didn't kill someone else and that you survived."

*I am.*

His boot crunched on gravel and his foot slipped on a rock. *Damn, better pay attention if I want that second kiss.* Putting his hand out to catch himself against the tree, he missed, his arm dropping forward. He rested on his cane, his other hand on his knee.

"You have to come all the way back by yourself too," Delia shouted.

"I know that, damn it."

"What'd you say, darlin'?"

She used that faux Southern Belle voice as if they were actors in one of her Broadway plays. "We're in the West, not the deep South. You sound silly," he said.

"I'm practicing for when you sweep me off my feet and smack a big wet one on me."

Jett let the cane lean on the side of his leg, took out the handkerchief from his back pocket, and wiped the sweat from his brow.

"Prepare to swoon." The words came out gruff and he cleared his throat.

Today, at the public tour of Mercy Mountain Lodge his family hosted, he got a kick out Delia being back for another visit to Colorado. She kept appearing in the last year at key moments. Like a guardian angel.

*A cheeky, slightly impulsive, and jaw-dropping sexy angel.*

"Do you need an incentive?" Her voice met him smooth and silky as he straightened again and headed back along the dirt path.

He didn't look up, instead keeping a careful eye on his shuffling feet, his dress boots gathering dirt. "You know what I want," he growled.

*I want to kiss you and I want this torture to end.*

He glanced her direction as she slid the V-neck of her dress to one side and flashed him one of her breasts.

*Is that a nipple?*

He picked up his pace. Sweaty and sore, he finally arrived in front of her smiling face. She stood on her tiptoes to kiss him on the cheek.

"That is not the kiss that counts," he said. "I'm not collecting a proper kiss for my efforts out in the open."

"I never think of you as shy. So where are we going, partner?"

She had switched to more of an Annie Oakley voice and he shook his head. It amazed him how she made a career on stage out of all that corny stuff.

"Come on."

He gave her his arm and she bore some of his weight. Her breast rubbed against his bicep as they walked back toward the big canvas tents. He lifted his chin toward his pick-up parked separate from the rest of the visitors' cars in the grassy field.

"Let's go to my truck." Under a tree. Private. Out of the July sun.

"Your truck?" She dropped his arm and stepped away. "You think I'm some hick that wants to make out in a truck?"

He smiled wide, knowing that would get her New York sensibilities in a twist.

"Why not? You've been talking like one for the last twenty minutes and flashing your legs and breasts at me."

"I'm trying to encourage your recovery."

"Well, honey, you did." He ambled toward the truck and threw his cane in the back bed with a loud clatter before opening the door and gesturing for her to climb in.

"Seriously?"

"I'm going to kiss you, Delia, but I'm not doing it on display for half of Ashnee Valley."

He waited, watching her mind appear to tick through options, then hid a satisfied grin when she climbed up. Holding onto the side of the bed, he made his way carefully around the late model truck before getting in on the driver side. It was surprisingly cool inside, so he slid the bench seat back and left the tinted windows up.

"Give me a minute." He put his head back on the headrest and closed his eyes, peeking out sideways to see if she bought it.

"Your eyes are open, so you're either dead or faking this tuckered out thing." She faced forward, her hands resting on her lap.

"Come on then." He chuckled, sliding his hand behind her, and scooting her body next to his. *Ouch*. "Let's get this over with."

"Let's get this over with. Really? I can refuse. It's not like we shook on it or signed a contract."

He pushed her honey-blonde hair off her shoulder and leaned in, running the tip of his nose along the rim of her ear.

"I like when you leave only a sliver of hope for me to work with. You do want me to kiss you, don't you?"

He understood she was only in the truck out of curiosity just like he was. To see if the same bolt of lightning struck a second time around. He ran his fingers along her collar bone, picking up the small diamond necklace she wore and letting it drop back on her chest. He loved the way the material of her dress, whatever it was — *satin* — locked her breasts together and pushed them high.

It took all his effort not to let his hand slide into that V, taking one of those magnificent globes into his possession, bringing his mouth down to suckle.

*Why not?*

She told him he could kiss her, and it wasn't like they'd agreed on the details. He sat back.

"What?" Her gaze followed his, down then up. "Oh, no, that is not part of this agreement. You are not kissing me…my…wherever. I know your reputation. I know how your mind works, thinking there's a penalty flag or a quarterback sneak you can throw."

"You got those game plays down good." He nodded while somehow managing not to scoff at her messed-up football lingo. "Sounds like you have me all figured out too, huh?"

"I'm from New York."

Jett took one of her hands and raised it to his lips, kissing her knuckles. "Damn, woman, your hands are cold. What's up with that? It's eighty degrees outside."

*Is she nervous?*

"Hey." He put his finger under her chin. "We don't have to do this. You got me walking a good distance. That was your real motive. It was tough, but I did it. I wasn't sure I could." He tipped his head to the side. "So, thank you. Come on, we'll go back to the party. No harm done."

This was not at all going the way she wanted. Jett opened his door, making moves to get out of the truck. Delia grabbed his arm and tugged her way right back against his side.

"I finally got you right where I want you and you're trying to get away?"

Jett closed the door again.

*He really has no idea what that cocky smile does to my insides.*

"Kiss me," she said dramatically.

"Who were you imitating then?"

"Ingrid Bergman. *Casablanca.*"

Jett shook his head. "I'm not here to kiss her."

"I know. I do better when I pretend to be someone else." Delia glanced at Jett's raised eyebrows then squeezed her eyes shut. "I'm not doing any of this right."

He tucked her hair behind her ear and ran his fingers along her jaw. She bit the inside of her cheek as if she'd sucked on a lemon.

*Good Lord, I'm salivating.*

"Look at me," Jett said. He put a warm hand to her cheek, guiding her to face him.

For how tan his skin was, she'd never noticed the sprinkle of tiny freckles over his nose. His dark brown hair, usually a bit more tousled, had been neatly combed for the benefit of the partygoers today. She glanced at his kissable mouth, his lips edging at the corner into a sly smile.

Jett leaned forward barely rubbing his lips to hers.

"Problem is," he said when his nose bumped hers, "I don't want to kiss anyone but you, Delia."

His ragged breath tickled beneath her jaw before his lips skimmed her cheek.

*Kiss my neck.*

Her eyes fluttered closed. His teeth nipped her earlobe before he sucked it into his mouth. She whimpered softly.

"That's it," his deep voice rumbled. "Now say it again. This time as you. Only you."

Oh, she wanted to, but it could lead to all sorts of things she wasn't sure how to handle. Another hot, brief, disappointing encounter. Wasn't that how all her dalliances with men ended? This man was everything to avoid, not the least of which, a recovering alcoholic. As if her mother hadn't cured her of ever wanting to be around another one of those.

*It's only a kiss.*

"Say it." His tone grew more demanding as he pulled her against his chest.

Finally, his kisses traveled along her neck. An insistent thumb brushed the smooth material of her dress, raising her nipple to a peak.

"Kiss me," she whispered pressing her body against his chest just as a knock at the window slammed reality to the front.

"No." Jett tightened his hold before a second knock followed and he hung his head. "If that's my brother, I will kick his ass."

"Hold on," Delia said, scrambling back to her side of the seat and silently blessing the universe for dark windows.

"Ready?" Jett asked before opening his window. "Hello?" He glanced at Delia with a shrug. "I don't see anyone."

He leaned farther out the window then suddenly drew back against the seat as a short, brown-haired woman dressed in a navy-blue suit moved into view.

"Who are you? What are you doing?" Jett asked.

"I'm sorry to startle you. Your brother said I'd find you here. My name is Rachel Linman." The woman offered her hand to shake. "I'm from Child Support Services. I need to speak with you about RJ."

"At a party? On a Saturday? What kind of crazy idea is that?"

Delia set her hand on Jett's arm. "I'll head back to the lodge."

"Wait. You can hear anything she's got to say. Go ahead, lady. Say what you need to say."

Rachel Linman put her hands on the edge of the truck door and stepped up on the runner, her head so close to the interior of the truck, even Delia pulled back.

"That's better. Mr. Mannis, I'm here because RJ's mother would like to see him."

"Hell no, she abandoned him and took off. I didn't even know I had a son. I'm still waiting on the paternity test report, but you probably already know he looks exactly like me. He's with me now. No way."

"I have the results." Pushing a brown envelope through the window, the woman stepped down. "He's your son, Mr. Mannis. I'll give you a minute to look over the papers."

Delia picked up her wilted bouquet from the floor of the truck. "I really feel like I should go."

Jett choked back a laugh. "He's my boy."

She touched the edge of the envelope. "Don't you want to open that up?"

"I'll look at it later." He leaned out the window. "Come back here. What'd you say your name was again?"

"Rachel Linman."

"Thank you for this, Ms. Linman," Jett raised the envelope in the air. "But my answer is the same. There's no chance in hell Annie's seeing RJ."

Ms. Linman stepped onto the runner again, leaned her head to the side to peer around him, and repurposed her displeased frown into a bright smile.

"Hello, we haven't met. I'm Rachel and you are?"

"Delia. It's good to meet you."

Jett looked from one woman to the other. "Uh, that was nice, but what's going on here?"

"Is there somewhere the three of us could talk? Somewhere more comfortable. Perhaps one of the picnic tables closer to the lodge would do?" Ms. Linman asked.

Delia adjusted her dress again. "This seems like something you and Jett should discuss alone."

"Can you give us a minute?" Jett asked and Ms. Linman stepped away from the truck.

"Come with me." His eyes pleaded with Delia as a he spoke in a low voice. "I need a friend who's thinking clearly with me on this one. I could use your help."

She glanced at the woman waiting patiently. "Okay."

He held her hand as they followed Ms. Linman, and each took a seat at one of the tables set up for today's event. Over the sound system echoed Ben's announcement to the crowd that the tour would be starting at the main lodge. For now, with everyone indoors, they had a perfect place for a private conversation.

"Mr. Mannis, your ex-wife, Annie…"

"She was never my wife."

"I stand corrected. My mistake."

Delia fidgeted in her seat, flustered at the firmness of Jett's admonishment while at the same time admiring the other woman's complete lack of defensiveness. It must be why Ms. Linman could handle a difficult job such as this.

"RJ's mother contacted us recently and she would like to see him. Normally, there would be more red tape to this sort of thing, seeing as she abandoned him, as you pointed out."

"I would hope so," Jett said.

Delia nodded when he glanced her way for confirmation.

"Where is Annie?"

"We're not sure exactly. The phone number she called from does have a Colorado area code. In any case, there are extenuating circumstances, and we're hoping you will be willing to work with them."

Jett frowned. "What kind of extenuating circumstances?"

"Well for one, you have only now been officially verified as RJ's father, not just a temporary custodian. We look at what is in the child's best interests."

"He's been with me and my family for months."

Jett stood and limped a few feet away from the table, carefully bending to pick up a couple wayward popcorn boxes underneath one of the tables.

His random movement to busy himself by picking up garbage confirmed Delia's hunch of his acute discomfort with the situation.

"I suppose this is where the red tape comes in?" He tossed the items into a trash container.

Delia patted his chair. "Sit down, let the woman explain." She took his hand when he sat, intertwining their fingers.

*What role am I playing now? Doting girlfriend?*

This would be a better impression than some random woman nearly straddling Jett's lap. She centered her energy and leaned in.

"Ms. Linman, tell us what we need to do. Why does RJ's mother want to see him? How can we help?"

"We can start some paperwork right now. Annie is no longer able to look after RJ on her own. She wants to make sure he's going to be taken care of during the time she has left and after she's gone."

"That's bullshit. She wants to see him and then leave again? How is that good for RJ?"

"Annie is very sick, Mr. Mannis. She's dying."

"Oh please." Jett leaned backed and crossed his arms. "She's playing you or something."

Ms. Linman tapped her pen on the folder in front of her. "You do understand I'm here for a purpose, and it's not the party you're having today."

Delia was unable to stifle a tiny cough at the curt remark.

Jett glanced at her. "I know, right? Can you believe this?"

"Annie *is* sick," Ms. Linman said, her voice rising in a distinct tone of disgust. "She's provided confirmation from a doctor. That's why we want RJ situated and all documentation in order. There is an importance to timing, Mr. Mannis."

She opened a folder in front of her.

"At least you're married now." Head bent, she shuffled through the papers. "That certainly helps with the appearance of this entire situation."

"Married? What the hell?"

His question seemed directed toward Delia, who vigorously shook her head, stopping short when Ms. Linman glanced up.

"Married." Delia stood, walked to the other side of the table, and sat next to Ms. Linman. She made her expression reflect what she imagined to be matrimonial ease.

"That's helpful?" Delia picked up one of the papers and studied it, hoping to demonstrate genuineness.

"As I mentioned, our top priority is always what is best for the child. Saying that, the court can still be conservative. Cautious. Things will go far more smoothly with a stable relationship, a stable household in which RJ is already living. His mother's history of drug abuse and Mr. Mannis's DUI…"

Ms. Linman patted Delia's arm, leaving her hand resting there. "Let's just say you may be the linchpin that holds this whole thing together."

*Oh shit.*

"We're not married," Jett said before she could stop him.

"You're not?" Eyebrows raise, Ms. Linman turned to her for an explanation. "Why not?"

"Why not, indeed!" Delia put a hand on top of Ms. Linman's and conjured up her best conspiratorial look. "Rachel, can you believe I can't get this man to take time away from his physical therapy to marry me? I'm about to book two flights to Vegas. Isn't that right, sweetheart?" Delia got up from the table, again standing behind Ms. Linman and slightly out of view.

A grin as wide as Wyoming spread across Jett's face.

"Actually, I had a surprise for my future bride before we were interrupted," Jett drawled.

*What the heck is that? His impression of a southern gentleman?*

"I was only a matter of seconds away from letting Honeybee – that's what I call my intended – know that I have everything arranged so we can be married in a week."

His smoldering look indicated he was half-way to the honeymoon. Delia rolled her eyes and moved around the table to sit across from Ms.

Linman again.

*I'd never circle the table this many times in a performance. I seem nuts.*

"That's so romantic and modern. You're a lucky woman. He's taken care of all the wedding details." Ms. Linman clasped her hands in front of her on a swoon-worthy sigh. "We can certainly work with this."

"Let's fill everything out as if you're already married," she said, looking down at her papers again. I'll file them as soon as the ceremony is over."

*Wait.*

Jett's big hands settled on her shoulders with a squeeze, his warm breath brushed her ear. "Hang with me. I'll figure our way out."

A half hour later Ms. Linman left with her forms and a reminder to let her know when to submit the paperwork.

"What did we just do?" Delia asked as they walked up the hill toward the lodge together.

Jett put his hand up. "Nothing we can't fix. The questions were mainly about me if you noticed. All she suggested is the more stable the environment is for RJ, the better." He paused then said with a silly grin, "I'm RJ's father."

"You're right. Let's focus on how amazing that is. Now you know for sure." Delia smiled. "How do you feel?"

"I feel great." Jett's expression turned serious. "Plus, terrified like when I first found out about him. I was still drinking then. It was just a few days before my accident."

"How long were you and Annie involved, if you don't mind my asking?"

He stopped walking and rubbed his chin with his thumb, looking everywhere but her direction.

"One night," he answered. "Listen, I know we're becoming better friends, and we have fun and flirt around with each other whenever you visit… but I'm not necessarily the nice guy you think I am."

She faced him. "Ah." She nodded.

*There is something dangerously appealing about vulnerability wrapped around a repentant man.*

"Then? Or now?"

"Let's just say, crashing my truck and breaking several bones in my body are the best things that could have happened to me. It put me on the straight and narrow."

"That's a pretty dramatic way to go about it." Delia said.

"I've been blessed with a second life, and I'll do whatever it takes not to screw it up."

"I admire your determination. You remind me of my dad. RJ's lucky to have you as his father."

"Thank you."

"I'm sorry to hear Annie is so ill."

"I'd spare RJ the pain of losing her if I could." He shook his head. "I was nine when my mother died. You mentioned your dad, is your mom still alive?"

"She's gone now." Delia tossed her drooping bouquet in a nearby trash barrel. "Should we catch up to the others?" She gestured toward the lodge as a group descended the front steps. "Looks like the tour is over."

"Yeah. We're all meeting up at Jim and Sofia's to debrief on the event and have some dessert."

Delia took his arm when he offered and walked toward the crowd.

"Way to raise a girl's heart rate, by the way. I can just see the marquee now." She swiped her hand over an imaginary sign. "*Instant Family* starring Delia Kincaid."

"Mrs. Delia Kincaid Mannis." He glanced sideways. "I should be so fortunate."

## Chapter 2

AN HOUR LATER THE FAMILY gathered at Jim's house and unanimously agreed the event at Mercy Mountain Lodge was a smashing success. Several people in town booked reservations for relatives for the December holidays when rooms would first be available.

Jett peeked around the corner into the bathroom as four-year-old RJ giggled then straightened his back as he stood on top of the toilet seat, Delia's hand on his arm.

"Repeat after me," she said. "A gentleman cleans up if he misses the bowl."

"A gentleman cleans up if he misses the bowl."

"And he always washes his hands."

"And he always washes his hands." RJ saluted.

"At ease soldier."

Jett took a step back, out of view.

"Come on, I'll give you a piggy-back ride to the kitchen. Your cousin Suze is waiting for you." Delia softly grunted when RJ's weight settled on her back.

"Are you going to tell my daddy?"

Her dramatic sigh drew a panic from RJ who started jabbering nonstop.

"I won't do it again. I was in a hurry. I had to go bad. You're so pretty, Miss Delia."

Jett shifted the toothpick in his mouth from one side to the other. *Nice save.*

"I see the apple doesn't fall far from the tree. You're sliding RJ, get your butt up there or this piggy-back ride isn't going anywhere."

"Ooh, you said butt. Butt is a bad word. I won't tell on you if you don't tell on me."

His little boy sure worked hard to avoid trouble, making him question if he'd been too tough on him in the short time they'd spent together. He cleared his throat and stepped forward as they exited the bathroom.

"Get on down, RJ, and run along. I need to speak to Delia about her language." He winked at her when RJ let go of her shoulders and slid down her back, landing with a thud on the hardwood floor.

"Are you going to hit her?" The boy bit his upper lip with his lower teeth, his big brown eyes full of tears. "It's my fault."

He got on one knee, holding RJ's upper arms.

*What has this boy been witness to that made him ask such a thing?*

"Have you ever seen someone get hit?"

"Yes."

"Did you see someone hit Annie? I mean your mother?"

"Yes."

"I would never hit Delia or your mom or any other woman." RJ's chin dipped. "Look at me, RJ. Do you understand? I would never hit. It's wrong. I would never hit you either."

"Yes, sir." RJ nodded. "A gentleman cleans his pee off the floor, and he doesn't hit."

Delia practically knocked Jett on his ass as she dropped to her knees and hugged his son against her.

"You are the smartest little boy I've ever met." She sat back on her heels. "I like you so much, RJ."

"I like you too," RJ said. "You smell like vanilla ice cream."

"Speaking of ice cream, Aunt Kai is serving dessert in the kitchen," Jett said. He sat on the floor in the hallway as RJ took off around the corner. He rested his aching back against the wall. "Lord help me, my son is a flirt."

Delia sat next to him, slipping off her heels and tucking her legs underneath her skirt.

He would have expected her to worry about keeping her dress clean.

"He made you blush," he said, studying her profile.

She glanced down, fingering the beading at the hem of her dress. "He's a little man full of contradictions, isn't he?" She lifted her finger to her lips and tapped.

His eyes followed, imagining their almost-kiss earlier in the day. Like a bee drawn to a flower, he breathed deeply, taking in her scent. The woman did have a tempting vanilla aroma.

"How is he a contradiction?"

"Well, he's clever and handsome and funny too."

"And that's a contradiction because?"

"Because he carries pain."

He leaned his head against the wall. "I don't know much about his life before I got him. It's coming out in dribbles, like just now. I wish I knew the best thing to do for him."

Rising to her knees she startled him with a fierce expression as she poked her finger hard into his chest. "You don't drink again, Jett Mannis. Ever. That's what you do."

Shocked by her sudden harshness, he grabbed her wrist as she added another jab. When she attempted to stand, he tugged just enough so she lost her balance and landed on his lap. By the way she squirmed it was the last place she wanted to find herself.

Her eyes narrowed. "Let go of me," she said, her tone dangerously calm.

"You aren't going anywhere until you tell me what the hell just happened."

The memory of her mother hit tangibly. Ferocious and fierce, like a cyclone. As if she haunted the hallway with her sickening perfume and the stinging slaps she delivered. Delia clamped her lips together as blood rushed through her ears.

*What happened to me as a child is nobody's business.*

"Are you going to tell me what that was all about or not?"

"Not." She scrambled off Jett's lap as heavy footsteps headed their direction. Closing the bathroom door, she rested her forehead against it, listening to the short exchange between Jett and his brother.

When their voices eventually faded, she inhaled a shaky breath. Tears stung as she walked the tiny bathroom in circles before sitting on the edge of the tub, her head in her hands.

*Why is this happening again? I thought I was done with these panic attacks. Mom isn't here. There isn't anyone to be afraid of.*

She stood and jumped in place trying to expel more jittery energy. Facing the mirror, she pinched her ghost white cheeks until color returned.

*Okay Delia, you're going to walk through the kitchen, smile big at all the Mannis family members, grab your purse, and go straight out the back door.*

"Excuse me, I need to make a quick phone call," she whispered, practicing with a happy wave.

Delia straightened her shoulders, vigorously shook her hands, and reached for the doorknob.

"Hey, everybody." She zoomed past the full table in the kitchen and waved with both hands. "Ice cream. Yum." She scrunched her nose, threw in a cutesy wink, picked her purse up from the counter, and kept on walking. "Is that my phone I hear ringing?"

"Jett, did you upset Delia?"

She paused next to the backdoor, listening to her best friend, Sofia's, accusation.

"That's a panic attack."

"I'm going after her," Jett said.

She opened the door when spoons clattered in bowls and chairs scraped the floor.

"No, you're not." Sofia's voice rose in volume. "I'll handle it."

Tucking her purse under her arm, Delia ran down the steps and through the yard until she arrived on the other side of a small barn. She checked for ant mounds, then sat in the grass breathing in the fresh-cut smell.

Less than thirty seconds after, Sofia rounded the corner and sat next to her. "I'm here."

"I grabbed my purse so I could call my dad," Delia said as she pulled blades of grass one by one. "I can't talk to anyone but him. Or you. This hasn't happened in so long. It used to happen all the time."

"I know. I was there, remember? Did Jett say something to upset you?"

"Yes and no."

"I knew it."

Delia playfully threw a clump of grass at Sofia and her protective certainty.

"Hey!"

"I hope you didn't make it worse, Sofia. Did you tell everyone my mother was a drunk?"

"Of course not. But you know diplomacy goes right out the window when it comes to you."

Sofia scooted closer and put an arm around her shoulder. "Remember when I kicked Charlotte Hinkey in the shin for making fun of you in junior high? You give the word, and I will tear Jett up."

Delia laughed. "I know you would. You're like a tiny whirlwind. Always there to look after me." She ran a blade of grass above her upper lip and scrunched her nose and lips trying to keep it there like a mustache.

"Jett's not to blame," she said when the blade slid off. "It's about RJ more than anyone else."

"Ah," Sofia said. "Now who's being the protective one? Is that what triggered the attack or did something more specific happen?"

"Something happened." Delia started ripping blades of grass into tiny pieces, the majority boomeranging back onto her lap when she tossed them in the air. "Clearly I haven't put my past to bed."

"Maybe it is time to work things through." Sofia gently smiled at her. "With some help. I know some great therapists in New York and here."

Delia shook her head and stood, straightened her dress, and brushed her hands along her bottom. She turned her backside to Sofia who responded to the gesture with reassurance.

"You're good, no grass stains." Sofia stuck out her hand and Delia pulled her up.

"I may have found a better approach," Delia said. "A crash course. More my style."

"What does that mean?"

"There was a woman from Child Services at the party today. She talked to Jett, well us, about RJ's mother."

"Was that the woman in the blue suit? She stuck out by the way she was dressed, but I didn't know who she was."

"Yes. She mistakenly thought Jett and I were married." Delia scrunched her nose. "She thinks we're getting married."

"What?"

"Her name is Rachel Linman. I guess RJ's mother contacted her agency and she's sick."

"Who's sick, Annie?"

"Yes. Very sick, not-going-to-make-it sick."

"That's awful, but it helps explain, sort of, why she left RJ the way she did and took off. Why did marriage come up in all this?"

Delia sighed. "It was a wrong assumption when she saw the two of us together. She said Jett's being married would make RJ's custody situation go more smoothly. It looks better, a more stable home life for the boy."

"And the two of you didn't correct her?"

"No. And I'm starting to wonder if it's not such a terrible idea."

Sofia lowered her chin. "Because…?"

"Because I know what it's like to be the RJ in this scenario. I know what it's like to have a parent die. So does Jett for that matter. Because Jett is still getting himself literally and figuratively back on his feet."

"Is it also a way to escape New York and the stage? You've been wanting a way out for a long time."

"It could be." Delia put her hands on her hips. "I'm exhausted and I'm not getting any younger. Who knows, maybe I'll want to sing again someday, but acting, it's a grind. I don't enjoy it anymore. You seem so happy here."

Sofia's expression reflected utter contentment. "I am. It's very different. Slower. Simpler. I love it here."

"That's what I want. Plus, I adore RJ. I love being around him." She put her hands over her heart. "Even more, I love who *I am* around him."

"That part I understand one-hundred percent," Sofia said.

"Here comes your husband, by the way. What is it he calls you when you get angry?"

"The Italian Prizefighter," Jim answered as Sofia spun around to face him. "Sorry to interrupt the conversation."

"Sounds about right." Delia suppressed a grin as Sofia straightened and her neck turned blotchy. "I heard you before I left the house, tough girl. Jett is part of your family now and he's your friend. You probably owe him an apology."

"Everyone inside is concerned," Jim said.

Delia put her hands on Sofia's shoulders giving her best friend a gentle push toward Jim, who opened his arms to hug her.

"Are you okay?" he asked her over the top of his wife's head.

"Yes, thank you." Delia shrugged. "Just a little drama from the actress, it's to be expected."

"You can stay with us tonight if you prefer. It's close quarters over at the cottage with Jett and RJ. We can re-arrange things, move people around between the ranch and our house."

"That won't be necessary but thank you. Besides, I'd break RJ's heart if I don't stay with him."

Sofia disengaged from Jim's arms and hugged Delia. "Let's talk more, okay? I love you."

"I know, silly goose, and I love you too. I'm okay. Now, go apologize to your brother-in-law so he can take me back to the lodge."

Delia followed Jim and Sofia to the house.

"She's my best friend," Sofia offered as her apology to Jett, who stood inside the family room, brow furrowed, arms crossed.

"I was worried," he said. "Is everything okay?"

"I'm fine now," said Delia. "Sorry if I scared anyone."

Jett stared at his brother. "Are any of you going to tell me what's going on?"

"Why are you looking at me?" Jim slapped a hand to his shoulder. "I don't have a damn clue."

The soft glow from the porch light barely lit the way two hours later as Jett carried RJ to his truck. After hugging the others goodnight, Delia followed with her suitcase and overnight bag.

"Are you sleeping over, Miss Delia?" RJ's sleepy voice trailed back toward her, his head resting on Jett's shoulder.

"Yes, I'm staying with you tonight."

In fact, she'd only be one bedroom away. While construction on the main lodge had been completed, the rooms were unpainted and unfurnished. Only one of the eight cottages on the property was ready to be occupied. It just so happened to be the one Jett and his son were living in temporarily.

RJ lifted his head. "I want to have pancakes in the morning and go swimming."

Jett patted his son's back. "We can do that, buddy."

"Will you go swimming too?" RJ's chin rested on Jett's shoulder as he spoke to her.

"You bet," Delia answered without hesitation. "I'm all yours."

Jett turned with a wink. "Lucky devil."

The truck had barely made it to the main road when she turned to the backseat and found RJ sleeping in his booster chair, his head leaning to the side and a little forward. Dark brown hair like his father's hung in his face.

"You have a wonderful son, Jett. The freckles across his nose are so cute. I adore all those wavy curls. I could gaze at him all night."

"He looks like I did at that age. My hair curled when I was younger too."

"What I want to know is how a body goes to sleep that fast?"

She studied Jett's profile as he drove, the few and far between streetlights allowing only fleeting glimpses of his handsome face. A dark shadow of stubble roughened his jaw line.

"He has nightmares."

"He does?" She turned to look at RJ again. "Poor little guy. What do you do when that happens?"

"I sing to him, rock him back to sleep."

Delia rested her head against the back of the seat. "That's sweet. What do you sing to him?"

He glanced her direction as they passed Patsy's Diner, the hot pink neon sign lit against the darkening sky.

"Songs my mother used to sing to me. It's funny how all the words come back."

"Mmm." She closed her eyes, letting the truck's motion rock her in its peaceful rhythm.

A tender brush of his fingers on her cheek awakened her when they arrived.

"Looks like I may have two people to carry in and tuck into bed." Jett chuckled.

In the middle of the night, Delia sat straight up in bed, swung her legs over the side, dashed to the door, and ran toward the terrible cries. RJ thrashed on his mattress, his eyes open, tears running down his cheeks. Jett rubbed his hands up and down RJ's little arms.

"It's okay. I'm here. You're okay."

Delia crawled onto the bed, inching close so she could run her hand over RJ's hair.

*What is happening in there that is so scary?*

"Sing to him," she urged, and Jett pulled his son onto his lap, rocking him. She didn't know the song, but the tender melody quickly soothed the boy's anguish.

Delia shifted closer, sitting in the middle of the bed with her hand on RJ's head. She wrapped her other arm around Jett's waist, resting her head on his shoulder.

*The man can sing.*

When RJ's breathing steadied, his little chest rising and falling rhythmically, Jett laid him back down. After covering his son with the blanket, he motioned for her to follow him into the hallway. He closed the door and took her into his arms, one hand against the back of her head, his other arm wrapped around her waist, holding her to him. She could feel his heart race.

"He's okay now." She leaned back, looking up. "Are you?"

"Let me get my bearings."

"Come on. We'll get some air."

She took his hand and walked to the door leading to the small patio, opening it a few inches. A cool breeze fluttered against her skin. Behind her, Jett put his hands on her shoulders. His chin rested on top of her head.

"Does this happen every night?" she asked.

"No, maybe once a week."

"I don't think he woke up at all. Does he remember the episodes in the morning?"

"Not that I can tell." He took a step back. "Thank you.

"For what?" Delia slid the door closed and locked it.

"You're always here when we need you. It helps."

"You're welcome. I'll do anything for RJ." She patted his arm. "I'm going back to bed. Are you staying up for a bit?"

"No." He rubbed his hand on his neck. "I'm going back to bed too. I'll keep my door open so

I can hear RJ if he has another nightmare."

"I'll do that too," she said as they walked toward their bedrooms.

## Chapter 3

IN THE MORNING, JETT OBSERVED his son falling hard for his first crush. RJ kneeled on a stool next to Delia as she added chocolate chips to the perfect circles of batter in the pan. He barely stopped chattering and only to hang on her words as she taught him the fine art of flipping pancakes. He listened as she told RJ about how he would one day make pancakes for his wife, his children, and his grandchildren.

How she imagined things so far in the future, Jett couldn't understand. Right now, it was enough for him to not drink, lead construction at the lodge, and take care of his son.

*One day at a time.*

"After pancakes, we'll go swimming." RJ clapped his hands.

They shared a look of amusement at the boy's infectious laughter. He rubbed his hand over his heart at a fleeting glimpse of joy. A sensation he still wasn't quite used to.

*Sunday morning peaceful.*

*Delia in a bathing suit.*

He'd bet money he wanted to go swimming even more than RJ.

Delia opted for a smoothie instead of pancakes and went to sit on the patio, saying she'd join them at the pool after her morning meditation.

He made RJ wait the requisite thirty minutes after eating before changing into their suits and heading to the pool together.

Having the small pool available was a bonus for the family to use while the lodge wasn't open yet. RJ stuck his toe in the cold water, crossed his arms over his chest, and shook his behind.

"I'll jump in first and then you can," Jett challenged as RJ shook his head. "Come on now, we're going to act like the water is warm when Delia shows up."

RJ wore orange-sherbet colored swim trunks and hopped from one foot to the other, giggling, with his hands in front of his mouth. "You mean like a riddle?"

"Not exactly, more like a practical joke."

Jett jumped straight in, sank to the bottom, pushed off to surface, and whipped his hair to the side.

"We'll joke her." RJ clapped.

Jett put his arms out. "I'll catch you."

With no further hesitation, RJ leapt into the pool.

*Have I ever trusted anyone the way this boy trusts me?*

They splashed and played in the shallow end, tossing a yellow plastic football. All the while, Jett remained aware that he and RJ both waited on Delia's arrival, as if the fun wouldn't really begin until she made an appearance.

Maybe she really was the linchpin like the Child Support Services lady suggested. He shook off the thought. Best to forget all that. Delia would leave in a few days, and the reality of proving he could be a responsible single parent for the long term would begin in earnest.

"She's here, Daddy."

The energy ratcheted up when RJ came splashing toward him in a frenzied rush. Jett picked him up and he latched on, cupping his hand around Jett's ear.

"We're going to joke her." RJ cringed in a spasm of giggles and Jett rolled his eyes.

Delia stood at the side of the pool with a suspicious smile and hands on her hips.

"What are you guys up to?"

She untied the belt of her cover up, revealing a small white bikini.

*Holy shit.*

Jett blinked in stunned delight at the exquisite woman with graceful legs, six-pack abs and the face of an angel standing before him.

"What?" His voice sounded gruff when RJ whispered in his ear, interrupting the fantasy he was having.

Delia raised one eyebrow.

"Put me up on the edge, Daddy. That way Delia and me can jump in together."

"Delia and I," she corrected. "I'm not sure about jumping. This bathing suit could come flying off and I'd be nekkid." The silly twang she added to the word naked sent RJ into another giggle spasm.

*Please jump.*

"You boys aren't trying to trick me, are you?"

"No, ma'am." RJ scanned back and forth between them. "The water's warm."

"Uh huh. Is that what you say too, Jett? The water is warm?"

He tore his eyes from the little triangles covering her breasts.

"Damn, woman, look at you." The words escaped before he could edit.

RJ slapped a hand over his mouth staring with wide-eyed delight at his dad's use of a bad word.

"On that note…" Delia pinched her nose, shouted "…cannonball!" and splashed into the water.

After an hour of Marco Polo, monkey-in-the-middle, and some spectacular handstands if Delia did say so herself, the three of them hiked, exhausted, back to the cottage.

RJ didn't fight the suggestion for a nap after Jett kept him awake long enough to consume a peanut butter and jelly sandwich and a big glass of milk for lunch.

"If you don't mind watching him for a minute, I can go pick up some salads from the diner for us."

"That sounds good, thanks."

"We can sit on the patio when I get back."

"Ok." Delia exhaled when Jett finally pulled a t-shirt over his head to go with the jeans he had changed into when they returned from the pool. His parading around shirtless for the last hour so distracted her, she'd dropped the jelly knife twice before getting it into the dishwasher successfully.

"See you in a few," Jett said and closed the door behind him.

She combed the tangles from her hair as she looked in the bathroom mirror. She wondered what it might be like run her fingers along the taut muscles of Jett's back. Or along the noticeable scars on his shoulder from the accident.

Walking down the hall, she peeked in the bedroom when RJ called her name.

"You're supposed to be sleeping, silly-head, what are you doing awake?"

He pointed to the desk. "Daddy's phone is buzzing."

"Oh okay, well you go back to sleep. I'll put your dad's phone in the kitchen."

"Will you lie down with me?"

"Do you promise to go to sleep?"

"I promise."

She took the phone into the other room, glancing at a message from Rachel Linman. Apparently, the woman worked on Sundays too. She set the phone on the kitchen counter, picked it up again her finger hovering to swipe, then set it down.

Coming back to the bedroom, Delia lay down and spooned RJ, her arm resting over his small body, her nose in his chlorine-smelling hair.

"Go to sleep," she whispered.

Jett found them wrapped up in each other's arms, asleep on his bed. He padded back to the kitchen and put the salads in the refrigerator, noticing his phone on the counter. Two missed calls from Rachel Linman.

He picked up the throw blanket from the couch in the living room. After spreading the blanket over Delia and RJ, he took his place on the other side of the bed, removing his t-shirt before he lay down.

*I could use a nap too.*

The kid exhausted him. It took a different kind of energy to keep up, but he couldn't imagine his life without him. He glanced over his shoulder at Delia with her long eyelashes and the slightest pink to her cheeks and wished she nuzzled that close to his neck. Turning over toward the two of them, he put his hand next to where hers rested on RJ's hip. Now the three of them were connected.

An hour later he shifted and opened his eyes to find Delia looking at him. She kissed RJ's cheek.

"What are you thinking about?" he whispered.

She took a quick look at RJ, then back to him. "That this little boy is so wonderful. It's overwhelming."

"Rachel Linman called," he said.

"It rang when you were gone so I put your phone in the kitchen."

"I better return her call." He groaned as he moved off the bed. "Keep RJ busy if he wakes up and I'm not off the phone."

"I will."

Delia snuggled back up to his son, and he questioned if it was normal to feel jealous of a four-year-old.

Back in the kitchen, he pressed redial and waited three rings before Ms. Linman answered. As he listened, shame crept up the middle of his back like a suffocating vine heating his skin. He didn't want this. To have to deal with Annie. A stranger. A one-night stand while drunk.

After the call, he stood in the doorway to the bedroom and gave Delia a thumbs down when her eyes questioned.

"Come back." She patted the mattress.

"Annie's coming," he whispered, settling on the bed with his back to her, not wanting his apprehensiveness on display.

She put her hand on his shoulder. Maybe she too wanted to connect the three of them through touch like he had needed earlier.

"Jett, I think we already know what would be best for RJ."

He turned over at her words. "What are you saying?"

Delia sat up and gestured for him to follow her to the other room.

"What do you want most for your son?" she asked once they were settled on the couch.

*The best. The best of me as a dad. To have a mom his whole life.*

"I know what I don't want. If Annie is this sick… I don't want him to grow up with her loss as his only experience of a mother. I know too well what that struggle is like. He needs a mom and a dad he can turn to."

"I'm sorry you lost your mom when you were so young. I want what you want for RJ too," Delia answered. "I'd like to help."

"It's always great when you visit. RJ can't get enough of you."

"Maybe there's something more I can do."

"You're not suggesting what I think you are." Jett stared at her, curious. "Are you?"

"I could be."

He pulled his chin back. "We would get married?"

Delia nodded. "What do you think?"

"Do you mean just while I'm getting everything settled with Annie?"

"Not exactly." Delia lifted a shoulder. "We could parent him through a first year together and then…" she shifted to face him head-on "…we could figure out what the arrangements look like going forward. It's a bit old-fashioned, but it would be better like Ms. Linman says if we're actually married."

Jett chuckled. "I'd finally look like I made a smart decision for once in my life."

"In all seriousness," Delia added, "if it came to it, lots of couples decide to co-parent and they're successful. Even friends."

*If it came to it. There's the out. Or there's a sliver of hope she's leaving. For me? Or maybe I'm hearing what I want to hear? Would I want that?*

"You'd be giving up more than I would. New

York. Your career. Are you sure you're ready for that?" he asked.

"I won't be leaving anything or anywhere I hadn't already decided to. Beyond that, I'm surprised to be saying any of this."

"I'm not exactly known as the poster boy of good behavior in Ashnee Valley," he said after a minute of silence between them. "I've cashed in all my chits with people in town over the years."

He tilted his head side-to-side. "Not showing up for work, not paying my own way. Outside my family, there aren't many who would give me the time of day and they wouldn't be wrong."

He studied the floor.

"There have been a lot of women, Delia." He glanced up. "You'd be gaining my reputation."

She bit her bottom lip. "If we were in New York all this could be the reverse."

"You have a sordid past too?" Jett chuckled.

"I imagine a small town knows all your business. Still, I've had more than my share of short-term relationships and with famous men. Well…" she rolled her eyes "… semi-famous. There's big town gossip too."

"Short term relationship. Is that what they call a one-night stand in the city?" He grinned.

"We both know what we're talking about."

"I know."

"This *would* be a marriage based in love," Delia said. "For RJ. For better or worse, in good times and bad, in sickness and in health."

"Until death do us part?"

"We'd have to be that serious about a commitment to RJ regardless of what happens between the two of us. Now it's my turn to ask you, would you be ready for this?"

*Don't fuck up the best thing that could ever happen to you and RJ.*

Jett took a deep breath. "For RJ, absolutely. It's hard to describe how much I want to give him a good life."

"We'd need to let the family know right away," Delia said. "And plan a trip to New York to visit my dad, but that's probably better afterward when everything's a done deal. We could start with telling Sofia and Jim."

He shot her a pained grimace. "And here we were having so much fun. Telling anyone else will be easier than telling my brother." He paused. "We'd really do this? That means in the next few days, you know."

Delia nodded. "Maybe we should sleep on it?"

"Good idea," Jett said with a broad grin. "But I couldn't sleep now if you paid me. Could you?"

"I may never sleep again."

They stared at each other for several seconds until she shrugged. "Should we sit outside and eat our salads now?"

He laughed. "Good idea. He stood and put his hand out to pull her up. "Come on."

She followed him toward the kitchen. "I think Sofia will be excited for us."

He glanced over his shoulder with an amused expression.

"I know. Sofia's not one to hold back her opinions. It's never hard to tell how she's feeling."

"That's the truth." Jett opened the refrigerator and handed one of the salads to her. They walked back through the living room and outside to the patio to sit in the sunshine.

"We're doing the right thing," Delia said.

"I agree." Jett lifted his gaze to her. "It's going to be good."

"Right," she said and dug her fork into her salad ignoring the roller coaster drop from her stomach.

# Chapter 4

"OF COURSE, SHE'LL MARRY FOR him." Sofia stomped her foot and threw her hands in the air. "He's adorable. I'd marry for him too."

"Aw shucks, baby girl. Does your husband know how you feel? It sure is flattering." Jett squeezed Delia's hand as they sat on the couch at his brother's house the next afternoon.

"I hate when you call my wife baby girl," Jim said.

"We all know I'm talking about RJ." Sofia sat down on the couch, taking Delia's other hand. "Let's discuss this more."

"They're adults," Jim said.

Sofia put her arm around Delia, anchoring herself.

"Sofia, don't start a tug of war."

Sofia tugged Delia a little further from Jett. "Do you love him?"

"Way to deal with your wife, bro." Jett laughed.

Jim ran his fingers through his hair. "You have

a lot to learn about marriage."

"Do you love him?" Sofia asked again.

"Yes," Delia and Jett answered simultaneously.

"We love RJ," Delia said, "so we've agreed to get married. That way RJ has support from both of us."

Jim cleared his throat. "You're taking on a lot more than RJ with this deal. That selfish bastard comes with him. You do understand that, right?" Jim grinned when Jett flashed his middle finger.

"Perhaps that part hasn't sunk all the way in." Delia bit her lip and glanced at Jett, the heat of the exchange drawing Jim's slow whistle.

"Don't encourage them," Sofia said.

Delia patted Jett's knee and stood. "Come on, Sof, let's you and I go for a walk."

"Take your time," Jett added. "We're heading over to the ranch to see Dad. We'll be back in a few hours."

The full-sun day made the dirt road blinding as Delia and Sofia walked in silence. After a short while, Delia put her arm around her oldest and dearest friend and squeezed.

"I love you. You crazy ass…"

Sofia hip-checked her. "Don't say it."

"Beyotch." Delia took off at a run with Sofia chasing after. She circled back seconds later, her arm resting again around Sofia's shoulder as the two let their breaths return.

"Why are you marrying Jett?"

Sofia's exasperated tone made Delia laugh.

"I think you're more shocked by the idea than I am. Let's get to the creek first and sit. I want to let my toes dangle in the water. It's so hot." She side-stepped down the grassy bank that edged the shallow water and sat.

Sofia slipped off her sandals, dipping her toes in in the water. "Oh, that's cold." She pulled her feet out at the shock before putting them in the creek again. "It feels good."

"So, is it me or Jett you don't approve of?" Delia asked.

Sofia turned toward her with red-rimmed eyes. "That's not fair. You know I love you both. And RJ. I just didn't think you were serious."

"Come on, I know." Delia scooted close and hugged her. "It's nothing to cry about. You're really upset about this, aren't you?"

"I understand you want to do this for RJ," Sofia said without making eye contact. "That you think this is best. But you're marrying a man you hardly know. He's a recovering alcoholic, Delia. Doesn't that scare you? It does me. I'm scared for you."

Delia sighed, picked up a stone, and tossed it in the water. "I may not know Jett well, but we are friends. This is for RJ." She glanced at Sofia's profile then back over the water again.

"It's for me too. I want more. A new life. I said that to you even before you left New York and that's almost two years ago now."

"And you can have a new life. You could take a break. Don't perform. Travel. Do things you've always wanted to do."

"This *is* something I've wanted to do. I've always wanted a family. A child." Delia splashed her toes in the water. "Do you ever feel like maybe what happened to you as a kid was meant to happen? Maybe my mother being who she was is so I could show up for RJ now? I understand from experience what that little boy needs."

"He needs stability. It's taking everything Jett can muster to recover from the car accident and stay sober. Are you prepared to put yourself in the role of mother and wife? Because that is real life, not some performance you can walk away from after ten weeks. Believe me, it will get tough."

Delia pressed her lips together and breathed out through her nose before turning to face her friend.

"Stop judging me, Sofia Madonna Pavarotti Russo!"

Sofia spurted laughter at the ridiculous name Delia used whenever the mood in their friendship required adjustment.

*I want to come to this spot with RJ and watch him run along the rocks. I want to enjoy the sun sparkling on the water.*

"We've talked about a trial run for a year. I want to help RJ and Jett. I can work on this fear I've had my whole life because of my mother also."

"This is the crash course you were talking about?"

"Yes."

"I get it, I suppose." Sofia sighed. "It's likely Jett will want some level of intimacy. I highly doubt he'll be okay with having you so close and you simply mothering his son."

"I know," Delia said with a little shiver. She tapped a blade of grass on top of each toe. "I've never had a relationship that lasted more than a week or two." She stared up at the sky. "My father is going to have a cow."

Sofia snorted. "That's an understatement."

"Do you think everyone else will understand?"

"Who? You mean like friends in New York?"

She ran the grass between each of her toes one by one. "I mean people in Ashnee Valley."

"Listen, I'm the only one who gets to be judge-y in this town," Sofia joked. "I'll take care of anyone who even gives you a sideways look. Besides, nobody will know about the year part but me and Jim, unless one of you shares that information."

"You're right. The three of us will be making a trip to see my dad in person to tell him."

"I strongly suggest you marry Jett *before* you show up at your dad's house. Or in Manhattan for that matter. He is one fine piece of man. You'll be beating back both women and men with a stick if he's not already taken."

Delia brushed sand from her toes and laughed. "That's my future husband you're talking about, missy."

"Yes, well." Sofia tucked her hair behind both ears and stood. "No pussy-footing around, you're certainly getting yourself a handful." Sofia wiggled her eyebrows. "Or a mouthful."

"You did not just say that. Who are you?"

"Your soon-to-be sister, babe." Sofia put out a

hand to pull her up.

"You've always been that."

The men surrounded him at the well-used kitchen table at the Mannis ranch. His father, Ben, to the left; his sister's husband, Leo, and nephew Will to the right. Jim sat directly across from him. Leo shuffled the cards and dealt.

"So, you're ready to handle a son *and* a wife?" Jim ordered his cards without looking up.

"What happened to you saying we're adults?" Jett put down two cards. "Hit me."

"I said that earlier so Sofia wouldn't claw your eyes out. Besides, I meant that I'm an adult, Sofia is an adult, Delia is an adult…"

"I get the point." Jett threw down his cards. "I'm out."

"You can't fold like that in a marriage," Leo said and pointed to his seventeen-year-old son. "Listen up, Will, this is a teaching moment."

Ben chuckled and raised his hand. "No more teasing."

A lecture loomed and it annoyed the hell out of Jett to wait for it.

"You got more to say, Jim, say it. We don't need to pretend we're playing cards."

"If we don't play poker then we're just a bunch of silly little girls gabbing." Will furrowed his brow, concentrating on moving his cards around. "You're crazy, letting a woman control you, Uncle Jett, even if she is gorgeous."

"Read 'em and weep, boys." Ben spread his

cards on the table. "I can't think of anything finer than a beautiful woman having control of me."

"Grandpa," Will said, his cheeks turning red.

Leo snorted. "I second that."

"Third," Jim said.

"Fourth," said Jett.

Jim collected the cards while Ben pulled his chips forward. Jett put his hands behind his head, tipping his chair on its back legs.

*Here it comes.*

"Delia is a successful woman," his brother began. "She has a career in New York. Is it fair of you to ask her to give up all that to move to the middle of Colorado to help you raise your kid?"

"It was her idea." Jett sat forward his chair legs clunking on the floor. "Okay, fine," he said looking from man to man. "It was a misunderstanding, something that Ms. Linman from Child Support Services implied would help. She assumed we were already married. This is for RJ's benefit and so there aren't any issues with Annie. That's all Delia is agreeing to. She understands the stakes for RJ."

He glanced around the table again.

"Does she understand what else you might come to expect from her?"

"Fuck off, Jim."

"Hey, hey," Ben said. "Keep it clean."

"Not everyone has an appetite like yours," Jim continued. "Has one woman ever been enough for you?"

"Whoa, Nelly." Leo grabbed the stack of cards out of Jim's hand and wrapped a rubber band around them and stood. "Game's over. Let's go, Will."

"Dad, come on," Will said. "I'm old enough to hear this. Besides, everyone already knows about Uncle Jett's reputation."

Jett tipped his head at his nephew. "Kid, you are not helping. Go home."

Jim slid his chair back from the table and left through the swinging door to the living room.

With a sigh, Ben hugged his grandson and patted his son-in-law, Leo, on the back.

"Thanks for helping me clean the storm windows. Tell Kai I'll stop by tomorrow. I'll read some stories to the kids."

His father came around the table and rested a hand on his shoulder.

"Take a few deep breaths and meet me in the living room, son. We'll settle in so Preacher Jim can deliver the rest of his sermon. The sooner it begins, the sooner it ends."

He laughed despite the sour feeling in his gut. Alone in the kitchen, he rubbed his hands over his face. Suffering through a speech from Jim, or anyone, would have been his cue to exit in the past.

Jett walked to the sink, refilled his glass with water, and looked out the window at the grazing livestock in the distance.

His brother hadn't hesitated once in stepping up to look after RJ as Jett recuperated. More impressive, Jim stepped back allowing Jett to lead the construction buildout onsite. The least he could do now is show respect and listen.

Twenty minutes later, Jim finally shut up from his barrage of questions only because their father interrupted.

"Okay, Jim, you've said plenty. Delia is a lovely young woman. This is a bit unusual way to start out, but it's not anyone's decision beyond hers and your brother's."

Turning to him now, his father asked. "What's your plan for this marriage and your family, Jett?"

He sat forward, his arms resting on his thighs, hands clasped.

"I'll do my best."

He took courage from the nod his father gave.

"I haven't had a drink in almost a year and there haven't been any women. There won't be any other women than Delia. I'll respect my wife and take care of her, even if we don't start out with traditional love between us. What's most important to me is RJ having a dad *and* a mom to raise him. That's how I can best love my son."

He looked directly at Jim. "My plan is to grab onto this opportunity with both hands and make the most of it."

A day later, with RJ playing with his cousins at Kai's house, Jett listened patiently as Delia read a list of wedding plans. They sat in the dining room at the cottage. Delia kept her eyes glued to a small, spiral-bound notebook and checked off each item as she spoke.

"It will be a morning ceremony." *Check.* "Performed by a judge." *Check.* "Jim, Sofia, Leo, and

Kai can witness." *Check.* "RJ and Ben will be there too." *Check.* She closed the notebook with finality, laying her pencil on top and lifted her eyes to his.

"No reception. No wedding night. No honeymoon." *Check. Check. Check.*

He scooted his dining room chair with cringe-worthy scrapes across the floor until only the corner leg of the table was between them. With a sweeping gesture, Jett pushed the notebook aside.

"No way, Honeybee."

"Jett, our initial agreement is for a year," Delia said with an exhausted sigh.

"If we're doing this, we're not doing it half-assed." He sat back in his seat. "Let's compromise. We'll do the ceremony your way. Everything you said. But we can still have a little bit of fun."

She sat straight in her chair, appearing to brace herself for his next words.

"We can have a party to celebrate. And we damn well will have a wedding night. With just the two of us."

He pulled the notebook and pencil back, pushing it in front of her again. "I'll even let you write that in your little book."

He groaned when she stood and walked through the house and out the back door, leaving him no choice but to follow.

*Quit playing around, dumbass.*

"Delia. Stop."

The screen door slammed behind him as he followed her along one of the many paths on the

Mercy Mountain site. When she suddenly veered off onto the grass toward the trees, he had to jog to catch up. Every step of uneven ground sparked a tiny stab in his back. With a grunt he stopped and bent forward.

"Where's your cane?" she asked, walking back to him.

He smiled at her concern. "In the house. Can we stay on the path please? Come on."

She followed him as he made his way to one of the benches along the way. He gestured for her to sit before he knelt on one knee in front of her. He rested one hand on the arm of the bench, the other on the seat next to her.

"We can have a wedding night. You're my wife for as long as we're married." He tipped her chin back to him when she turned her head away. "I will have you as my wife in every way."

He groaned with an oath.

"That didn't come out right at all." Pushing on the bench to stand, he rubbed his hands on his lower back.

"I am not promising to have sex with you on our wedding night or any other night." Delia crossed her legs, bouncing her foot.

"I know that. If you'd let me explain, I was only going to suggest it should just be the two of us that night. Adults only. Before we launch into the rest of this new family life."

He sat next to her. "Give me a minute to say this." He ran his fingers along the stubble on his cheek.

"The chance you're giving RJ means everything. And the fact you're willing to do this for me too. It's way more than I deserve. I'm aware of that, okay?"

"I'm the one that suggested it, remember? I'm not doing this out of pity."

He smiled. "I appreciate that. It would feel like crap if you were. But beyond RJ, it's hard to understand why you would do this for a man like me."

She studied him. "You're very hard on yourself. Almost as if the last year of recovering and taking care of RJ don't count."

"I've had a lot of help from my family. One year doesn't come close to making up for the years of bullshit I put them through."

She shifted close and held onto his arm. "You're not used to how good the feeling is when people really want to help."

"I guess not." He chuckled. "I'm not used to people wanting to speak to me, let alone marry me." He sat forward so he could look in her eyes. "Let me give you a party after our wedding ceremony. Let RJ show you off a little. Will you let me do this? Please."

"I'm so nervous about what people will think. Everything seems such a big deal in a small town."

"A party is a great way for folks in Ashnee Valley to meet you and get to know RJ better. Besides, it will look good if we're celebrating in public."

"Okay, you're right." Delia nodded. "It's not like I don't enjoy a good party."

"Thank you." He put his arm along the back of the bench. "Don't forget you still owe me that kiss you promised too."

She poked him in the side. "You just couldn't stop yourself from reminding me, could you?"

He flinched and laughed. "Too soon?"

## Chapter 5

TINY WHITE LIGHTS SPRINKLED THE tall trees surrounding the northern edge of the Little Forest Fairgrounds, public property that butted up against the grounds of the lodge. A slight wind rustled through the leaves, and insects hummed.

Each table for the reception had a white spread with a white hurricane candle encircled by wildflowers as the centerpiece. Lawn chairs surrounded an enormous bonfire that already burned. A lot of preparation had gone into making their wedding celebration special.

"You did all this for us, for me?" Delia murmured. Jett cut the engine and got out, then headed around the truck to open the door for her.

He helped her down, watching the careful way she held the skirt of her robin's egg blue dress in one hand and his hand with the other.

"Everything I do from now on is for you."

He turned when RJ called, "Daddy", and ran

in their direction. He'd never tire of hearing that.

"And squirt here," he said as he scooped up his son.

*Oof, that might have been a mistake.*

He tickled RJ then gingerly set him down. "Can't have a party without my wrestling buddy, can I?"

He put his arms around Delia in a loose hug.

"The people of this town are going to descend on you momentarily and whisk you away for the next few hours. I know you're not used to being the center of attention." He chuckled when she gently slapped her hand on his back. "Let these fine people dote on you. You and RJ are their excuse for a party. Enjoy it."

His smile beamed when she looked up and nodded. Holding her cheeks, he kissed her. Slowly. Deeply. As if there weren't trucks and cars pulling into the parking lot. As if RJ wasn't tugging on his shirt tails. As if they were the last two people on earth.

"Mrs. Delia Kincaid Mannis."

"Jett" her voice wobbled, "don't make this more than it is."

"I don't remember promising to act shy around you. You're a stunning bride. It's hard to take my eyes off you." He ran his thumb along her bottom lip and whispered, "A year. I know."

He sensed the crowd moving in to surround them, the voices growing louder, a few wolf whistles teasing at the corners of their embrace.

"Even though we'll just have a quiet night, I still can't wait to be alone with you," he said.

Delia gave the performance of a lifetime under the constant heat of everyone's attention. Not a moment passed when Jett didn't seem to be watching her too. His smiling gaze followed her every move. It was the moments when he didn't smile, when his attention felt like a caress, that made her skin flush in response.

She searched for Sofia in the crowd. "Hold my hand," she said when she found her. "What am I doing?"

Sofia led them to a small table where they could sit and speak in private. "What's going on?"

"What am I doing about my wedding night?" Delia picked up her glass of sparkling grape juice and sipped. "What's my plan?"

She cringed to find Jett looking at her and hoped he didn't know how to read lips.

"Um, are you considering…jumping right in? Tonight?"

Delia stood then immediately sat down. "This is a totally insane situation."

"Is he pressuring you?"

"No. Not at all. In fact, he just wants a night with the two of us."

"That sounds kind of nice. It doesn't have to be anything more."

"Maybe it would be better to hurry up and get it over with. That's what I've always done before. What do you think?"

"I think you're working yourself up. Part of what you said you wanted was to slow down. To get past your fear. Of intimacy, right? There's no chance of intimacy let alone remaining friends if you start out with a fake performance."

"Right. I'm confusing myself with this party where I'm playing a role and real life where—oh my god, I'm really married."

"Yes, you are. Here they all come." Sofia squeezed her hand, pulling Delia up with her.

"Hey," Sofia said when Jim and Jett arrived with RJ. "Hi, buddy. Are you ready to spend the night with Uncle Jim and me? It's getting late but I think we could probably fit in a little cartoon time before bed if we get going."

"Okay," RJ answered.

"Say goodnight to your dad and Delia."

"Love you, RJ," Jett said. "We'll see you in the morning."

"Love you, Daddy."

Delia knelt to give RJ a hug. "Sweet dreams, RJ."

Sofia took RJ's hand. "Have a good night you two."

"Congratulations," Jim added. "Brunch at our house at ten tomorrow."

"Ready?" Jett asked Delia after the family departed. "There's a surprise for us back at the lodge.

The tent was twenty-by-twenty and sat on the grounds of the Mercy Mountain site, far from the main building. Soft yellow lights lined the path, and someone had sprinkled rose petals.

*Okay, Kai, that's a bit over the top.*

The tent could have been a permanent structure if the interior was any indication. A king-size bed, lamps, a small refrigerator, and a floor rug occupied the space. More tiny white lights draped the nearby trees and another campfire burned.

Jett held Delia's hand as they walked inside.

"Glamping. I love it." She smiled. "What about a bathroom?"

"Spoken like a true city girl. No bathroom. I'll walk you to the cottage when needed. It's not like I'm planning to get any sleep tonight."

He tapped the end of her nose, trying to wipe the wary look off her face. "I don't mean anything by that."

He couldn't get used to the idea that Delia could be this nervous. He'd seen the internet stories like anyone else. Her life was considerably more documented than the average person's. There wasn't a handsome actor she hadn't dated.

*She probably has more experience than I do.*

He mentally calculated the ten years he'd spent intoxicated and sleeping his way through the female populations of Ashnee Valley and the nearby town of Four Bears.

*Perhaps not.*

"You aren't concerned about being alone with me, are you? You've dated every eligible actor between New York and Los Angeles."

*Christ.* He could kick himself six ways from Sunday by the look she gave him.

"That was a stupid thing to say. I'm sorry."

She waved off his comment.

"This is amazing. Who set all this up?" Running her hand over the pale pink bedspread, she then picked up a stuffed purple unicorn. "Interesting choice here."

"Kai and Leo did it. Anything pink or purple would be my niece Suze's touch."

Jett picked up two glasses, opened the small refrigerator and pulled out a bottle of water.

"Do you want to sit by the fire? Look at the stars?"

His hand rested on the small of her back as they walked. She held their glasses as he arranged the lawn chairs closer to the small fire and gestured for her to sit.

"We can share a blanket this way," he said.

After several minutes of silence, Delia stated the obvious. "This is not a typical wedding night."

"No." Jett chuckled. "May I interest you, my dear, in a glass of sparkling water?"

Delia laughed. "That sounds lovely. Thank you." She took the glass he offered and a small sip.

"Would you like to hold hands?" She waited on purpose while he took his own sip before holding out her hand. "Husband."

He choked on a laugh. "Trying that word out?" He took her hand and sat back.

"Wife."

"Well, we did it." She sighed.

"Yup." He added a little squeeze to her hand. "This is nice."

On the tail end of a hiccup her first giggle erupted. She snatched her hand back and put her glass on the ground, then patted both her cheeks, trying to regain composure without success.

"Yup. Very nice." He repeated, laughing with her as she doubled over in a fit of giggles.

In the semi-darkness of the morning after the wedding, he opened his eyes to find Delia watching him sleep.

"Good morning," she said.

"What time is it?"

"Maybe five."

"Good." He grunted. "I need more sleep. Why are you awake?" He rubbed his eyes and turned on his side facing her.

"It's noisy out here in nature." She held her hand in front of her mouth as she spoke. "The birds are definitely up talking."

"Hold on." He rolled over and lifted a small basket from next to the bed. "Here."

Delia peeked in. "Breath mints? Wow, Kai thought of everything."

"Yeah." Jett chuckled. "She has a lot of plans."

"For us?"

He shrugged. "She's a romantic."

"I like that your family wants so much for each other." She popped a mint in her mouth and settled her head on the pillow.

"When you were a boy what life did you imagine for yourself?"

"That's a loaded question this early in the morning. Depends on what age. If we're talking teenage boy, I'd say this is close. Do you always look this pretty in the morning?"

"Mmm, interesting. We're very alike."

"What do you mean?"

"Flirty, making it about sex when things get vulnerable. I do the same thing."

He chuckled. "It's always worked in the past."

"I've exhausted myself on it." She lay on her back. "I can't turn my inner sex goddess on and off like a switch any longer."

He turned onto his back too and stared at the top of the tent.

"Okay, let's see. When I was little, I wanted to be a rancher, like my dad. I still do, I guess. We spent time together and he was teaching me about it. That all stopped when my mom died. Most of what I know after that came from Jim, but it wasn't the same. Jim wanted to leave here the first minute he could. I didn't realize it at the time, but he really got saddled with looking after me with dad being so depressed."

"Maybe you can teach RJ all the things you know." She rested her hand on his chest, and he covered it with his own. "It's not like you don't have access to the family ranch."

"That's true." He nodded. "What about you? It's hard to believe you don't want all the fame and glory of being an actress anymore."

"I liked a lot of it," she admitted. "I've enjoyed the attention—and the money. Hard work is a good way to make the time go by…and to hide."

Keeping a hold on her hand, he turned on his side again. "Is marrying me and being with RJ a new way of hiding?"

"It feels like the opposite. More like taking

steps to come out of hiding."

"Good," he said, lifting his hand to her cheek. "I like this you."

"I like this you too."

"This might sound a little crazy, seeing as we're married for reasons other than…"

"Love," Delia added. "It's okay to say it. If we're being real."

He hesitated. "This is hard to ask."

"What is it?"

"Do you think you could ever trust someone like me to be a real husband?"

She lifted her head, eyes wide at his question. "I know you're a good man."

"That's fair." He smoothed his hand along her hair. "Would I be a jerk if I asked you again if you're always this pretty in the morning?"

She brushed his cheek with a shy little kiss before moving away again.

"Why do you call me honeybee?"

"At first it was because of your honey-colored hair."

"And now?"

"Because when you hover close like you just did, my heart wants to know what it would be like when you slow down enough to land."

"What if I sting?"

He gave her a contemplative look. "Seems worth the risk to find out."

# Chapter 6

*Staten Island, New York*

IT BURNED JETT'S HIDE TO have to request permission from Rachel Linman to take his wife and son on an airplane to New York. As if the rights of a mother who abandoned her own son superseded everyone else.

So far, Annie was still a no-show in Ashnee Valley. He'd anticipated this possibility and never mentioned to RJ she might come for a visit.

RJ held his hand, skipping as they made their way through airport security for departure. He hadn't stopped talking since they got in the car this morning.

*Have you ever been on an airplane, Daddy? How does it stay in the air? Do you think I could say hi to the pilot? Can Mr. Cheetah come too?*

"Who is Mr. Cheetah?" he'd asked when they packed their suitcases the night before.

RJ held up a furry stuffed animal who'd seen better days. "My cheetah. Silly Daddy."

"Silly Daddy," Delia repeated with an incredulous look before side-stepping the playful smack on the butt he tried to give her.

He examined the titillating way she bent in front of him now as she took off her wedge sandals and plunked them in the plastic bin on the airport conveyer belt.

*Lord, she wears sexy shoes.*

"Are you hungry?" Delia looked between him and RJ.

"Huh?"

"I thought I heard your stomach growl, or maybe that was you?" She poked RJ in the belly making him giggle.

"I may have growled, but it wasn't my stomach," Jett answered. "I was hoping you would bend over and help me take my boots off." He grinned when she shook her head.

"Get all that…" she circled a finger at him in warning, "out of your system now. Before you meet my dad. He's a cop, remember? Plus, I'm very nervous about this trip." She whispered the last part so RJ wouldn't hear.

"That's why I'm trying to ease your tension." Jett stopped to raise his arms overhead for the security scan. "So, will you?"

Distracted with trying to help RJ put his shoes back on and gather her own items, she didn't answer him.

"No?" He prompted.

"No, what?"

"Bending over for me?" He raised his eyebrows. He enjoyed the tiny smile she tried to hide as she put the strap of her carryon bag over her shoulder.

"You're bad."

"You have no idea. Besides, you like it. I can tell."

His sexually charged words teetered on the limits of public conversation.

*This is too much fun to resist.*

"Admit it, you like me." He inhaled, suddenly more uneasy about how she might react than he wanted to be.

She gave him a bold look. "What if I do?"

"Don't tease me, now." He tilted his ego-swelled head.

He'd missed playful banter with a woman. He also enjoyed the return of his libido, which left the arena for months after his accident. Don't worry, his doctor told him early on. It won't be an issue long term.

*Thank God, because even if there's only sexy talk with my wife for now, this is my new favorite activity.*

"This is not the right time. You, sir, are no gentleman." She used one of her silly voices.

"I'm a gentleman." RJ jumped into the conversation.

Delia cracked up and put a hand on RJ's head. "Yes, you are, young man. You are a perfect gentleman."

*Foiled by a cute four-year-old.*

Once they boarded and were seated, Jett pulled his hat over his eyes and his big hands relaxed, one resting on each thigh. The man fell asleep instantaneously, before the plane even took off. It reminded Delia of how quickly RJ could fall asleep in the car.

She focused on pointing out things to RJ, describing what every sound meant as the flaps on the wings moved and the wheels came up after take-off.

Her nerves were worse than opening night as she rehearsed the news she would deliver to her father. She imagined he hoped someday she'd marry and have a family, but to find out after the fact could be an unhappy surprise to him. She'd reluctantly given over Jett's birthdate when her father asked for it. No doubt he'd run a thorough check and be armed with the facts about Jett's past transgressions including his DUI.

"What's Grandpa like?" RJ asked her when they'd reached altitude and leveled out.

"You have two new grandpas these days, don't you?" Delia smiled when RJ nodded and hugged his stuffed animal close.

"Well, he's nice like your Grandpa Ben. My dad was a police officer. He likes to play board games and card games, so that will be fun for you. His favorite thing is ice cream."

"Do you think he'll like me?"

"I know he will." Delia tussled his hair. "I called my grandfather Papa. So, I guess he would be Papa Jack in this case."

"Will we ride on the big boat to get to his house?"

"We'll ride the ferry tomorrow. We're going to

take a cab today. Do you know what the ferry is?"

RJ shook his head.

"It's a special boat that takes people back and forth between Manhattan and Staten Island. Lots of people ride the ferry to get to and from work each day."

"Will Papa Jack like Daddy?"

Delia peeked to see if she detected any sign Jett listened from under his hat. She went for honest.

"Maybe not right away, but he will eventually. I'm his only child and he's a protective father. He might have to get to know your daddy."

"Uncle Jim says Daddy takes getting used to."

Delia pressed her lips together, nodding at the wise-sounding sentiment coming from such a little boy.

"Could be."

When Jett used one finger to push up his hat, she shied away from his gaze.

*That wasn't a very nice thing to say.*

She finally glanced at him, her heart beating hard at his genuine smile. No more teasing or suggestive looks like earlier when they were playing around. Warmth spread through her heart at the thrilling sensation of true affection on his face. *For me.*

Delia considered how gross to think the exhaust fumes from the buses and taxis outside the terminal smelled homey. She managed to get through the airport with only two autograph requests but could tell it shocked Jett when a couple of middle-aged women stepped up to ask her for them.

A few people were taking pictures with their cell phones now when she followed RJ into a cab while Jett loaded their suitcases in the trunk. Sofia had warned her there were modest rumors on social media about her "disappearance," questioning whether she'd ever return.

*Does anyone really leave the Big Apple once they make it here?*

She wasn't exactly famous, but to anyone who frequented Broadway plays, she was easily recognizable.

In the cab, Jett reached across his son who sat between them and squeezed her shoulder.

"Don't worry. I'll work hard to charm your dad. I'm not using my cane in front of him either."

"You don't have to go that far."

"It's a guy thing. I need to wean myself off it anyway."

"Don't try too hard," she added. "And don't be disappointed if he's tough on you at first."

He looked at her with an expression of optimism. "As long as he's not tough on you, we shouldn't have any problem."

*That's exactly what I'm afraid of.*

RJ clung to her hand a short time later as Delia helped him out of the cab.

"This is Papa Jack's house?"

Jack Kincaid stepped onto his front porch. Her father had thick salt and pepper hair cut short, almost military short. He wore jeans and a gray t-shirt, looking younger than his fifty-five years with an athletic build maintained by daily runs and weightlifting twice a week. It was no surprise where her discipline for working out came from.

The Cape Cod–style house she grew up in had meticulously trimmed bushes in the front and perfectly edged grass. Dad kept up with the neighbors in competition for most manicured lawn. It shocked her when he'd suddenly started using organic fertilizer and putting up bird feeders a couple years go. He even let a few bushes behind the house grow downright unruly, enough to support a family of bunnies.

"It's important to leave an Earth worthwhile for the next generation," he explained at the time.

"There you are," Jack said. "Come on up here, kiddo, and bring all these folks you brought to visit with you."

"Hi, Dad." Delia made her way to the house as Jett picked up a cowering RJ and carried him up the steps.

"Dad, this is Jett Mannis and his son, RJ, short for Russell James."

"Welcome. Nice to meet you." Her father shook Jett's hand before turning to RJ. "Russell James, that's a fine name."

RJ pulled his stuffed animal tighter and shrunk away, his head tucked into Jett's neck.

"We're still working on the proper way to greet new people," Jett said with a chuckle.

"Looks so." Jack turned to head in the house and Delia winced at Jett's tight-lipped frown.

"Will you be staying here tonight or going straight into the city?"

"We'd like to stay the night, sir, if that would be

all right with you."

"That would be just fine." Her father walked down the main hallway toward the back of the house, speaking over his shoulder. "You and your boy can sleep in the den on the hide-a-way."

Jett put RJ down and closed the front door. "That won't work, sir, because I plan on sleeping in the same bed with Delia."

*Oh God.*

She closed her eyes as her father's footsteps rumbled back down the hall. He stopped in front of the three of them.

"Is that right?" He glowered over the top of his glasses.

"Yes, sir. It is."

"And why's that?"

*Oh crap.*

She glanced at Jett's expression as it faded from friendly to stubborn, then took RJ's hand. "How about I get RJ settled with a snack in front of the TV, and then we can go in the living room so we can talk. Dad, maybe you could get everyone some water?"

Her father's face darkened. He abruptly turned toward the kitchen as she pointed Jett toward the living room.

"I feel like I should be wearing a bullet-proof vest. You gave him some sort of head's up, right?"

"Um, not quite." Delia high-tailed it down the hallway with RJ in tow.

Jett settled on the couch and accepted the glass

of ice water his soon-to-find-out-father-in-law offered. The thought of spanking Delia's sexy behind distracted him until she returned, sitting next to him without making eye contact.

"I'm afraid there's been a misunderstanding, Mr. Kincaid," he said as he tried to take the lead.

Delia put her hand on his arm. "Dad, we wanted to visit and see you in person because we have some news."

She cleared her throat, declining when Jett offered his glass of water.

"Jett and I are married," she blurted. "We got married a week ago." Her voice rose an octave. "In Colorado. I'm going back. I mean, I'll be staying. There. Moving. There. Because we're married."

Jett took her hand as reinforcement, pulling his chin back when Jack Kincaid stood and flashed a fierce look then abruptly left the room.

"What the fuck was that?" he whispered to Delia. "He just leaves?"

The sound of a refrigerator door slamming and a can opening preceded Jack's return to the living room where he thrust a beer in Jett's face.

"I sure need a drink. How about you, son?"

"Dad!" Delia swiped the can away, sloshing half of it on the rug.

Jett involuntarily gripped Delia's hand tight. It wasn't his first instinct to stay seated nor calm if purposely provoked.

"Is this a test?"

"Yes, it's a test," Delia snapped. "You did a background check on him, right Dad?" She walked across the room and picked up her purse. "He knows all about your DUI. We're leaving. We'll go to my apartment. I'll explain in the cab."

The tension between father and daughter had the shape of an iceberg. No way in hell did he fly all the way to New York to see her dad, only to depart in the first fifteen minutes.

"Everybody, take a breath. Sit back down, Delia." He pointed to the chair her father previously occupied. "You too, sir. If you would? Let me check on RJ, then the three of us are talking this out."

Two minutes later, he found them stewing in silence exactly as he'd left them.

*I'm amazed one of these two hotheads hasn't already marched out of the room.*

"Show of hands, who understands that Delia's my wife?"

Jack stared straight-ahead and Delia gave a meek wave. A flash of movement caught his eye as RJ tore into the room landing with a smack against the side of Jack's recliner. He jumped with his arm in the air.

"I do! I was at the wedding! I want to play. Ask another one."

*This kid is adorable.*

He took in the gentle hand Jack placed on RJ's back to steady his enthusiastic boy.

"For the record, I only drink water now," Jett said.

"And coffee." RJ jumped again. "Do you drink coffee Papa Jack?"

"Papa Jack?" Jack looked to Delia, then patted RJ's shoulder. "Yes, I drink coffee."

"I got one." RJ waved his hand in the air. "Who likes ice cream?"

"He appears to be over his shyness." Jack chuckled. "RJ, how about you and I share a bowl of rocky road ice cream after supper? If that's okay with your dad and your, uh…my daughter."

"Take it easy, RJ," Jett said when his son started tugging Jack from his chair. He turned to Delia. "It's up to you whether we stay. We go where you go."

"We can stay." Delia sighed.

"I'd like that," Jack said. "And if we could talk more later too. This comes as a shock. I apologize for reacting so poorly."

"What's for dinner?" RJ asked oblivious to the awkwardness in the room.

Jack took RJ's hand and walked toward the kitchen. "What do you say we call the pizza delivery man?"

"Yeah, let's go call the pizza man!"

Her husband ran his fingers through his hair and exhaled in a slow, steady hiss when they were alone again.

*Her husband.*

"I'm taking our bags upstairs. I suggest you come with me. Now."

What had she been thinking? Jett had every right to be irritated with her. She could only imagine her father's disappointment. She sympathized with why he'd reacted the way he had, although she wasn't ready to forgive his outburst quite yet. Thank goodness for RJ and his ability to shift the axis of the earth with his exuberance.

She joined Jett on the upstairs landing, going first when he motioned her forward. For some crazy reason she imagined he might pinch her bottom as pay back so she jogged up the steps.

"That's Dad's office." She pointed to a room on the left before entering the last room on the right off the hallway. "This is my bedroom."

"Our bedroom." Jett kicked the door closed with his boot and dropped their bags on the floor. "And you are in so much trouble."

He stalked forward, with a wolf-like smile as she retreated. When the back of her knees met the bed, she sat.

"I'm so sorry."

Her heart thumped double-time when he put his hands on her knees and knelt before her, wedging his big body between her legs.

"*Now* you're sorry?" He tickled her waist, climbing on the bed, towering over her as she fell back twisting and turning.

"Uh oh, do you think dear ol' dad can hear the headboard banging on the wall? Want to get naked? That way when he busts in here, he can pull his sidearm."

"Stop." Delia laughed. "Jett, this is my childhood bedroom."

Climbing off the bed, he headed to the door and turned back.

"You snooze, you lose." He shrugged. "I'm going downstairs for pizza and ice cream. Besides, you're the one that gets to stay up all night talking it out with him, not me."

The next morning, Jack opened the back door for Jett.

"Come on out and walk the yard with me before you all head into the city."

"Can I come?" RJ asked.

Delia scooped him up. "I have something really cool I want to show you. It's in the basement. Do we still have that foosball table, Dad?"

"Might be a little dusty, but yes. It's down there."

Jett motioned her father to go first out the door. "My turn," he mouthed to Delia, pointing at her with a smack to his butt as if she were next up for a spanking. He observed the dark circles under her eyes and kissed her forehead to offer support. Turning around he absorbed Jack's glare over the top of his glasses with a don't-forget-who-I-am stance.

*Great.*

They slowly walked the entire yard, Jack naming particular plants and whether they had already bloomed for the season or would soon. Jett nodded, asking a question here or there, waiting for the moment he knew would come.

When his idiot brain considered how he kept finding himself on the receiving end of lectures these days, he snorted.

"I'm glad you find this whole situation funny," Jack said, stepping right up into his personal space.

*Here we go.*

"No, sir. Awkward, yes. Funny, no. I want you

to know I plan to take care of your daughter. I've been sober for a year…"

"Be quiet." Jack held up his hand. "There's a whole lot of things I can tell you don't understand."

*Jesus, this guy is a trip.*

Delia's father motioned for Jett to sit on the rock wall in the backyard, then took a seat next to him and sighed deeply.

"If I know my daughter, she did this…" Jack paused. "First, I admire that you're in recovery. Second, your brother is a good man. Jim is one of the best police officers I ever had the privilege to work with. That gives me some comfort here. However, there's one reason, and only one, why Delia would ever put herself anywhere near an alcoholic, let alone marry one, and that's to protect someone she loves. And by that, I mean RJ."

*I'm done with the "sir" crap.*

"Jack, your daughter and I are married. That's a fact. Period. We love RJ. And we care about each other."

"Care?" Jack slapped his hands on his thighs and shook his head before standing. "Do you want this marriage to last?"

*Thank God. Delia didn't tell him about the one year.*

"Of course." Jett settled in, watching Delia's father pace in front of him. "It's obvious Delia hasn't told me something you feel I need to know."

Jack scoffed. "My wife. Delia's mother was an alcoholic. The disease ravaged not only her body, but her mind until her death." He paused and took off his glasses. "I know it's a disease. A painful God-awful disease. My wife tried. I tried." Jack put his glasses back on and looked directly at him. "Delia suffered for it. I don't ever want to see her suffer again."

## Chapter 7

BIGGEST MISTAKE OF HIS LIFE. Worse, this marriage was the biggest mistake of Delia's life. As considerately as possible he'd suggested they annul this marriage sooner than later. She kept trying to convince him otherwise that night and the entire rest of their trip. Even during the flight back to Colorado, a day and a half later, she made several attempts to talk him down. When Jim picked them up from the airport, she still whispered hotly in his ear.

*Nope. Not budging. What more is there to discuss?*

"Go give your Uncle Jim a hug," Jett said as RJ took off running toward Jim's car.

"Did you have a nice trip?" his brother asked as he put their suitcases in the trunk.

Delia shook her head not even trying to hide the truth.

They settled in the car for the drive back to Ashnee Valley.

"Lieutenant Kincaid wasn't happy?"

"Funny," Jett mumbled.

Fortunately, RJ kept his brother occupied chattering about the museums they visited and the tall buildings while he and Delia sat in silence.

"Sofia has a late lunch waiting at the house for everybody, and Kai's bringing Suze over afterward for you to play with. How's that sound, RJ?"

His brother didn't wait for an answer.

"Then I'd like to hear some stories from your dad and Delia too. They've been awfully quiet so far."

At the house, Jett poked food around his plate as Delia spun a happy story about their trip. Finally, his brother offered an escape, suggesting the two of them take a quick horseback ride over to check on construction at the lodge.

"Hurry up," Jim called over his shoulder, en route toward the front steps to the lodge when they arrived.

"Keep your pants on. I've stopped using my cane and we did a lot of walking in New York. I'm beat."

"Sit." Jim held up two cigars. "Since we can't share a drink, how about a cigar?"

"Thanks, I appreciate the gesture."

His brother didn't really like cigars and more importantly neither did his brother's wife.

"Everything okay with you and Sofia, or are you looking for an excuse to be banished to the couch tonight?"

"She has cramps."

"Is that a pout?" Jett asked.

"You're the newlywed. How's your love-life going?"

Jim snipped the end of one cigar before trading out with Jett so he could prepare the second one. He leaned in when Jim held the lighter for him.

"You're taking a long time to answer the question."

Jett examined the cigar. "No sex and the trip sucked. I'm trying to convince Delia to get an annulment."

The shove and hard landing in the dirt at the bottom of the steps came as a surprise.

"Ow!" Jett held up his broken cigar. "What the fuck did you push me for?"

"You made this mess," Jim muttered, trudging down the steps and toward his horse.

Scrambling, Jett followed and hurled himself at Jim's back, tackling him to the ground.

*Shit, that hurt.*

He grabbed hold of his brother's belt and stuck his knee in his back.

"Aren't you going to make me listen to one of your bullshit lectures?" He panted the words in Jim's ear before landing with a thud as Jim flipped him. He rolled hoping to get away. Jim smacked a hand over the side of his face and mashed his head into the dirt.

"Get off me!" He stopped struggling until Jim pushed off to stand then hooked his foot around his brother's ankle and sent him sprawling.

*Take that.*

"Ow, shit," he yelped when Jim's boot crushed down on top of his hand.

Jim bent forward, breathing heavy. "Tell me you'll fix this."

"I can't fix it that easy." He squirmed and swung his other arm in another attempt to knock Jim off balance and failed. "Okay, okay. You win."

Jim backed off and Jet sat up, brushing dirt off his pant legs. He winced at the awkward angle of one of his fingers.

"How's your hand?"

"My pinky is dislocated."

"Pop it back." Jim grabbed his wrist and snapped his finger in place with a loud crack.

"Mother fuck!"

"You're welcome."

"You know we're lucky no guests are staying here yet. Dad would have our hides for rolling around on the ground like a couple of idiots."

"You started it." Jim laughed and sat on the steps again.

At times, Jett romanticized the notion of brotherly talks.

*Way less violent.*

When Jim left at eighteen for the service, he was twelve. Loneliness soon led to his numbing his feelings with booze to avoid suffering without his mom or brother, and his dad in thick denial.

*We've come a long way in the last couple years.*

He took a seat next to Jim and let out a breath. "It's complicated."

"I'm listening."

He rubbed his eyes, hesitating a moment about revealing what Jack Kincaid had shared.

"Delia's mother died from alcoholism."

"I know," Jim said with a sheepish wince.

"You knew? Did Sofia tell you? Of course,

she'd know."

"Yes."

His mouth tightened. "And you didn't think maybe *one* of you should have told me before I married her?"

"Sofia didn't tell me until after you two were on the plane to New York or I would have."

"Jesus, Jim." Jett pinched the bridge of his nose. "I wanted a mother for RJ, not me too."

"What do you mean?"

"It's pretty obvious she wants to protect RJ by keeping an eye on me at the same time."

Jim glanced his direction. "She told you that?"

"No. Jack basically did."

"What did he say about her mother?"

Jett sighed. "That she was verbally abusive. That Delia's panic attacks used to happen all the time. He says acting helped her cope. I just hoped…"

"What?"

"I thought there might be something more than just her feelings for RJ."

"I wouldn't count it out." Jim smiled with encouragement. "You two have a spark. That's for sure."

"You think so?"

*I sound like a thirteen-year-old girl.*

Jim laughed. "Maybe we can swap lip gloss tips after this."

"Shut up."

"So, you haven't slept together?"

"No." Jett groaned. "Remind me never to bare my soul to you again." He rolled his shoulders. "Besides, she says she's worn herself out on the whole sex goddess act."

"If it's been an act, then there's going to be performance anxiety involved."

"That's stupid."

Jim sat forward on the step. "Hear me out. Delia is an unbelievably good-looking woman."

Jett nodded. "She is."

"And famous, at least to people who like that sequined, let's-all-kick-in-a-row, sort of thing."

Jett snorted. "She's an actress, not a Rockette."

"You know what I mean," Jim continued. "Sofia says Delia has never had a real relationship. When she did date, it was a publicity stunt, or she was some celebrity dude's fantasy lay. That's pressure. You know, they say for women to have pleasure, it's all about what happens in twenty-four hours prior to the actual sex."

Jett stared at his brother's smug expression. "Where did you get that factoid?"

"Leo told me." Jim shuddered. "Don't think about Kai."

"This is the weirdest conversation we've ever had." Jett paused. "But there's more going on than just Delia's hesitation."

"Okay."

"I can't remember the last time I had sex sober."

"Oh." His brother rubbed his chin. "Ah." He nodded knowingly.

"What the fuck does that mean?"

"I don't know. I'm trying to show empathy. Have you talked with your sponsor about it? Is this a thing?"

"A thing?"

Jim rubbed the back of his neck. "What does it mean?"

"It means I don't remember shit." His voice rose. "I don't even remember sleeping with Annie."

Jim grunted. "It was once with Annie, years ago, and you were wasted. It doesn't make the best story, but the past is the past. You can't beat yourself up about it forever. You remember being with other women, right?"

"Of course." Jett rolled his eyes. "Not in detail. It didn't matter before. Now it matters. Or it would matter. With Delia."

"I get it. The stakes are high and you're unsure of yourself. So, don't rush." His brother put a hand on his shoulder. "I know I lecture you sometimes but try not to take the easy way out. Remember your plan to grab onto this opportunity."

"Is this where you tell me to be a man and suck it up?"

Jim scoffed. "No. I hate those expressions. This isn't about male or female. It's about seeing things through. Staying with it. It feels good, Jett, to see something through even when it's tough. Even if it doesn't work out exactly the way you wanted."

Jim bumped his shoulder against his. "I wouldn't have Sofia if I hadn't seen it through. It was you, when you were still in the hospital, that told me I was a chickenshit if I didn't go after her, remember?"

Jett laughed. "So, you've told me."

"You're a Mannis. You have this in you. No less than I do, or Kai, or Dad."

"Thanks, Jim. That means a lot coming from

you."

"Does Delia want to call the marriage quits?"

He shook his head. "No."

"Then it's settled. Come on. I brought something for you."

Jim led the way back to the horses.

"I need you to swear you're going to work things out with Delia first."

Jim held the envelope he'd pulled from his saddle bag out of reach.

"And as much as I am jealous of your fishing trips with Sofia, if you need to consult more with my wife about all this, I'll allow it."

"You'll allow it? I see now why you and Jack Kincaid got along so well." Jett made a grab for the envelope. "Give it."

Jim took a step back. "I'm serious, man."

"What's in the envelope?"

"A wedding gift."

Jett tilted his head. "With a big ass string tied to it. I can't promise I can make her stay after a year."

"But you're going to work on it."

"I am, but…"

Jim pushed the envelope into his chest. "Take it."

He ran his finger the length of the seal. "What is this?" He lifted his eyes to Jim in question, then pulled out a stack of papers held together with a binder clip.

"Dad signed over the property to each of us. You, me, and Kai. We're officially the owners of Mercy Mountain Lodge."

Jett grinned. "I guess I'll amount to something

after all."

Jim threw an arm around his shoulder and pulled him in for a hug. "Come here, this is going to be quick."

He slapped his brother's back. "Is that how you love on Sofia too? Come here babe, this is going to be quick."

Jim doubled over laughing. "Good one."

Jett rubbed his palms on the back of his jeans as he stood in the kitchen doorway. He should have more confidence after the talk with his brother.

"How about you leave the dishes and I'll do them after I give RJ a bath," he said to Delia as she collected dishes from the table and set them on the counter.

She turned. "Sounds good. I'll let them soak a bit."

"You could go soak in the tub too. We could meet back here in an hour and…visit."

"Visit?" She laughed and turned back to the sink, running the faucet, and waving her fingers underneath the stream checking the temperature. "That sounds formal."

He moved behind her as she squirted soap around the sink. Placing his hands gently on her, he massaged her shoulders.

"I want you to go take a bath now. Quit working so hard. It can't be easy the last couple weeks adjusting to a whole new life. Go soak and come back." He kissed her cheek and enjoyed the small shudder her body couldn't hide.

"I would like to *visit* with my wife after I get RJ to bed."

Delia squeezed his arm as she brushed by and headed down the hall. He listened to her making a pit stop to say goodnight to RJ.

Entering the second bathroom a couple minutes later, he found RJ running the water already.

"Little man, you know that's not allowed," he scolded. "Only grown-ups fill the tub."

RJ had a way of carrying himself, snapping his shoulders back when he didn't agree with something. It reminded Jett of his nephew Will, stubborn and determined to do things his own way. He made a mental note to catch up to Will soon.

RJ stood buck naked surrounded by dinosaurs he'd placed along the edge of the tub and stared up at him.

"I can do it myself."

"Maybe so, but it's not safe. You could turn the hot water on too high, and you're not allowed to be in the tub alone. Come on now, you know all this already. Don't test me."

Jett leaned forward and pushed one of the dinosaurs into the tub.

"Hey, those are my dinosaurs!" RJ pushed the rest of them one-by-one into the tub in a series of splashes.

"There won't be any space in there for you." Jett lifted RJ into the tub, the water only reaching mid-calf on the boy. "Make room so you can sit down. Oh hell, did you pee first?" How many times would he make that mistake only to have to start the whole bath process over?

"I peed."

RJ sat down and Jett kneeled next to the tub. He scooped water into a plastic sports cup from some forgotten baseball game.

"Close your eyes so I can get your hair wet." He dumped the entire contents on the boy's head, chuckling as RJ sputtered unprepared for the assault.

"Where's Mommy?" RJ asked as Jett rubbed in shampoo.

"Upstairs taking a bath."

"*My* mommy."

Jett paused his scrubbing, then resumed. He shouldn't expect RJ to think of Delia like a mom. He needed to slow down his own thinking too.

"Your mother is busy taking care of herself."

"Mommy's always sick."

Jett nodded. "She's not feeling well."

"Is she going to die?"

Jett rinsed his hands in the water before reaching for the cup.

*How do I answer that?*

"Close your eyes." Jett filled the cup and rinsed RJ's hair.

"Sometimes she can't get her medicine," RJ offered innocently.

He winced at whatever his son had possibly been exposed to. He set the cup of warm water down too hard on the edge of the tub, accidentally splashing water on the floor and his jeans.

"Damn it."

He pulled a hand towel from the bar next to

the sink and laid it on the floor.

Delia poked her head in the room. "What's all the swearing I hear coming from the bathroom?" She raised her eyebrows at her men.

*Her men.*

"Daddy said it."

She bit her lip so she wouldn't undermine the sweet wet-haired boy busy telling on his father.

"Well, enough of that language." She gave them both a stern look.

"Yes, ma'am." RJ offered in his sweetie-boy voice. Jett rolled his eyes as he brushed the towel around the floor with his foot to dry it.

"Well?" she asked Jett.

"Yes, ma'am," he agreed and leaned close. "You can put me in a time out later."

When Jett joined her on the front porch after an hour, Delia pulled her nightgown and robe tight around her. She wore an old-fashioned style that matched the setting as she stared at the rock formations known as Moonshine Ridge in the dwindling evening light. The air was less humid than summers in New York, and she appreciated not having to fend off mosquitoes.

"I won't ask," she said and tucked the long white gown under her toes and wrapped her arms around her knees.

"What?"

"About the man talk in there."

He grunted, stretching his legs down the steps, and reclined on his elbows.

She lifted his hat off his head, pressing her lips together when he pulled his legs back in and sat up again.

"Why'd you do that?" The deepness of his voice washed over her as he took his hat from her and tossed it on one of the chairs behind him. He scooted closer, his thigh resting next to hers.

"I don't know." Her skin tingled as he rested his hand on the middle of her back, making one big circle before holding steady again. "You're home. It seems like a man isn't really home until he takes his hat off."

"I was hoping you'd say it was so I could kiss you." His hand made another circle on her back, heating her skin beneath her robe and nightgown. "Can I kiss you?"

She barely nodded before he dropped a gentle kiss on her lips and pulled back to look at her. He leaned in again, his tongue drifting along the seam between her lips, desiring entry.

She wrapped her arms around his neck and ran her hand over the fine hair at the base of his head as she sunk into his kiss.

Sitting back, he moved a hand up one of her ankles and along her calf. "Why do you wear this getup?"

"What do you mean? It's a nightgown and robe."

"From the 1800s." He tried to separate her robe from her nightgown. "There are a lot of layers."

She swatted at his hand playfully. "What are you doing?"

"What do you think I'm doing? I'm trying to

get near some skin, woman. This is a ridiculous outfit. Don't you get all twisted in bed?"

"Would you rather I slept on the couch?"

"Hell, no. What do you have on under there? Pantaloons?"

Delia flushed. "No."

"That's all you have to say?"

"No underwear?" she added.

He laughed as he stood, pulling her with him. "Get your bonnet, baby. Let's go to bed."

Her heartrate quickened. "Wait."

"I'm beat, Delia. We're just going to sleep."

"It's not that." She put her hands on his chest, looking up at him. "I like this. I like how we're taking our time to get to know each other better."

Jett picked up his hat from the chair and opened the door. "I like it too."

# Chapter 8

TWO WEEKS LATER, JETT CHOSE a fishing spot for his sister-in-law to try where the Talking Fish River met Nicala Creek. Here they could sit on the ancient platform bridge and fish from above. Here he could ask his wife's best friend some questions.

"Everything okay, baby girl?" He put a hand on the wood platform, before lowering himself slowly.

"Yes, why do you ask? You're the one groaning, by the way. How's your back?"

Jett shrugged. "A lot better. It's just stiffness. Are you sleeping? You look tired."

He held Sofia's line, digging a worm out of the coffee can filled with dirt he set between them. Wrapping the worm around the hook, he took in the sigh and drop of her shoulders out of the corner of his eye.

"Jim and I were up late last night talking about your dad."

"What's going on?"

"He's been thinking about the future, it sounds. He and Patsy are serious these days. What do you think about him seeing her? Does it bother you?"

"About Patsy? I don't have a problem with it. My guess is she's been in love with my dad for a long time."

"He always worries so much about what you, Kai, and Jim think. I don't know if he'll ever forgive himself for falling apart after your mom died."

"I know." Jett rubbed his chin. "Does he want to get married again?"

"I think so. He doesn't feel he can run the ranch any longer. Patsy's planning to retire too. Don't say anything yet. He's only talking to Kai. She's been sharing a bit with Jim." Sofia shook her head. "Okay, none of this is why you got me out here, is it?"

"Not really." Jett let the line go and handed the rod back to Sofia. "I wanted to talk to you about Delia."

"What's she up to today, hanging out with RJ at home?"

"They're at Safety City. It's part of prep for starting kindergarten. She wants to do things with him on her own sometimes. I think it's a good idea."

Sofia glanced his way. "Me too."

Jett sighed. "I can't figure out why neither you nor Delia told me how her mom died. I had to get the story from Jack Kincaid while the guy practically wanted to tear me limb from limb for marrying his daughter."

Sofia let her line drop into the water below and follow the slow-moving current.

"I can't speak for Delia and why she didn't tell you, but my guess would be because she didn't want you to decide you wouldn't marry her. She really wants to be here for RJ and…"

He finished tying a fly and let his line drop in the water. "And what?"

"You're using a fly?"

Jett shrugged. "Want me to teach you to fly fish someday?"

Sofia rested her rod on her thigh and pulled the brim of her hat lower. "Definitely."

"There's a little more to it than the bait." Jett nudged her shoulder. "And what?"

"She married you for other reasons too. She's tired of New York. Tired of performing."

"I know that part. What else? Come on Sofia. This is like pulling teeth."

"Why?"

"I want to know more about what I'm dealing with here."

Sofia reeled in her line and dropped it again before answering. "Don't you think these are questions the two of you should have discussed before you got married?"

Jett ignored the dig.

"I heard from Rachel Linman again. Annie is coming into town this week, and we're setting up a time for her to see RJ." He rested his arms on his thighs. "I'm concerned about RJ, but Delia too. She's so open and loving with him. I know she's the mother he needs. She's the mother I want him to have. I want to know how to make her happy. Maybe we can last too, longer than the year she's agreed to."

"Really?"

"Yes, really. Why is it so hard to believe I would want that? I'm not the person I was before. I'm not drinking any more. I go to meetings. I'm working hard to make the family business the best it can be. I'm grateful to be alive. I've changed."

"Jett, you haven't changed, you're just being who you really are now. Without numbing yourself in alcohol."

"Delia loves RJ. Who knows, maybe she could learn to love me too."

"If only love were something we could conjure up. Are you saying you love her?" Sofia asked.

He lifted his hat and ran his fingers through his hair. "I don't know." He watched a dragonfly skimming the surface of the water. "I've never felt anything like I do when I'm around her."

"I worry you're playing with each other's hearts."

He repositioned his hat and squinted beneath the rim, letting the sting of his sister-in-law's honesty release on a ragged breath.

Sofia rested her hand on his arm. "I know this is for RJ. That's Delia's priority too. I'm acting like you need to prove yourself to me. I'm sorry. That's not helpful."

He lifted his eyes to hers. "I'd like to try with Delia."

Sofia nodded. "Is this what you and Jim talked about the day you got back from New York?"

"Sort of."

"It would explain why your fingers are taped together and Jim groans like an old man every time he sits down."

Jett grinned. "Maybe."

"Do you two ever have a conversation that doesn't amount to an argument?"

"Not really. Your husband is a hothead."

"You two make me miss my brother."

"From what you've always said, Anthony was way smarter than us."

"He was." Sofia set her fishing rod down, making sure to tuck it under her thigh to keep it from falling off the bridge. "He and Delia were close too. He was the only man besides her father she felt safe with."

"Did she tell you that?"

Sofia gave him a sad smile.

"What Delia will always want is the ideal family, the one she never had growing up. She also wants a real relationship. Until she fell in love with RJ, I don't think she thought any of that would ever be available to her. She certainly isn't going to easily believe she can have it all. And for all Mr. Kincaid's gruffness, he's a great father. Her mother was not a nice person. My brother and I witnessed just enough to know that when we were growing up."

"She says she feels like she's coming out of hiding."

"That sounds promising."

Sofia grabbed her rod again and gave it a hard tug, setting the hook.

"Got one," she said and reeled in her catch. "Even though Delia is my best friend, that doesn't mean she's told me what it was really like for her at home. I'm not sure she's ever told anyone. I'd keep giving her time."

"Look at you." Jett said proudly, eyeing the fish she pulled from the water. "Angler extraordinaire."

"I have a great teacher."

Jett met Rachel Linman mid-week in a conference room at the social services building downtown. He'd left Delia and RJ at home for this first meeting with Annie. Unable to sit still, he paced, glancing out the window and rubbing his lower back.

"Are you still in physical therapy?" Ms. Linman asked as they waited for Annie to arrive.

"Yes. I'm able to do some weight training now. I can't really do any cardio like running." He glanced her direction. "Too jarring."

She nodded. "I enjoy step aerobics. It's low impact on your joints."

"Yeah. I won't be doing that."

Ms. Linman laughed then pushed back her chair at the knock on the door right before Annie entered the room.

"Annie," Rachel said. "Come on in." She held out her hand in his direction. "You know Jett, of course."

Annie wore sunglasses so he had no idea if she even glanced at him.

"Hi," she walked into the room and set her purse on the table.

Jett didn't respond, instead trying to recollect anything about this short skinny woman with wavy brown hair. *Nothing.*

When she'd left RJ with him months ago, it had been the middle of the night. She had a friend with her, and it all lasted about five minutes before she took off. That sounded crazy to him now as he thought back on it. An angry heat raced up the back of his neck.

"Here, have a seat," Ms. Linman offered to Annie. "Jett, would you join us? We can get started."

Annie took a seat kitty-corner to Ms. Linman and took off her sunglasses.

He sat down at the far end of the table, his eyes meeting Annie's for the first time.

*Those green eyes.* Jett focused on twisting the silver wedding band he wore. *I remember.*

He lifted his chin. "Hello, Annie."

"Thanks for seeing me. How is RJ?"

He nodded. "He's doing well. He's fine."

Her shoulders relaxed and she smiled with a glance to Ms. Linman. "I can't wait to see him."

He bristled, turning his neck to the side, but didn't say anything.

"That's what we're here to talk about today," Ms. Linman said and started pulling papers out of a folder in front of her. "To begin –"

"Hold up a second," he said. "How are you feeling?"

"Me?" Annie put a hand on her chest as if startled. "Not so good."

He studied her gaunt cheekbones and the peculiar orange tint of her skin. At first glance someone might think she had a deep tan. Her arms and hands were the same color.

"I'm sorry you're ill."

"Me too." She kept her eyes fixed on the table in front of her.

"I'd never know about RJ if you weren't sick though, would I?"

Only her eyes ticked up. "No."

Ms. Linman fidgeted in her chair. "Let's not get off to a bad start. We're here to discuss visitations with RJ."

"You can't see him alone," Jett said.

"Mr. Mannis," Ms. Linman said. "That's not how this works."

"I'm okay with that," Annie said, catching him off-guard with her quick response. "But," she continued with a sneer, "I'm the one dying, so maybe you can drop the attitude and give me a fucking break."

*Nice.*

"No." Ms. Linman put her 'stop' hands up with a don't-push-me glare at each of them. "That's not how this is going to go." She put a piece of paper in front of each of them. "Read that and let me know if you can both agree to it. It outlines how visitations could work. It's a starting place and we can discuss changes either of you would like to see."

Jett picked up the paper and sat back in his chair. Out of the corner of his eye he scrutinized

Annie as she read.

"I can agree." She put the paper on the table. "And I don't need to see RJ alone. If you're there," she glanced toward Ms. Linman, "or you," she gestured his direction. "I don't care. I want to see my son."

Jett's whole being begged him to leave the room. He shifted in his seat and read the paper for a second time.

"I'd like to speak with my wife before I agree to anything."

"You're married?" Annie asked.

"Yes." He turned to Ms. Linman. "I also want to ask a friend of mine to help. You may know her. Her name is Cindy Wheeler.

"I know Doc Cindy."

"Who is that?" Annie asked.

"She's a psychiatrist in town," Ms. Linman answered. "I'm sure she would be helpful to all of you."

"I know you want to see him." He spoke gently, tempering his crossness to gain her cooperation. "Would you give me another few days to talk to my family and make arrangements, so Dr. Wheeler is there the first time RJ sees you again?"

She gave a curt nod. "Rachel knows where I'm staying."

"This may not feel like progress," Ms. Linman said. "But progress has been made."

In an odd moment of synchronicity, both he and Annie said, "uh huh" at the same time.

His eyes met hers. "Thank you."

"Let me know when and where. I'll be there." Annie put her sunglasses on and walked out of the room.

Late the next morning, Jett passed Gordy's Hardware store as he walked to Dr. Cindy Wheeler's office. The Thursday lunch crowd hustled full swing in downtown Ashnee Valley. He nodded at the walkers with their crisp white tennis shoes getting in exercise before going back to work. Other people ate at outdoor tables or picnic-style on blankets near the river that ran through the park in the center of town.

Doc Cindy, as everyone in Ashnee Valley called her, had to be the most styled woman he'd ever met with her signature pantsuits, trendy hair, and impeccable jewelry choices.

More important he trusted her. Before sobriety. Before his accident. From the moment RJ first appeared in his life. She'd been solidly there for him.

He passed Café Lilly and did a double take at Cindy sitting with his brother, Jim, and Jim's buddy, Rafe.

"Hey," he said coming up to their table. Cindy blocked the sun with her hand and looked up at him with a warm smile.

"Hi, Jett. How are you? Would you like to join us? Grab a seat."

"Here." Jim wiped his mouth and stood. "You can have mine. I need to stop at the Queen Bee Bookstore and pick up a book Sofia ordered before I head back."

"Thanks," Jett said and sat down. "I was hoping I could catch you for a few minutes, Doc."

"Sure," Cindy said. "I'm almost finished. Do you want to talk here or go to my office?"

"Here's fine." He nodded at his brother's best buddy from his Army days. "How are you doing, Rafe?"

"Good, man," he said as he brushed crumbs from the front of his University of New Mexico t-shirt.

"You coming?" Jim asked Rafe.

"Nah, I'm good." Rafe thanked the young waitress who placed a slice of blueberry pie on the table in front of him so slowly it was obvious she hoped to catch his eye. "Oh," Rafe said after Jim had left, "unless you wanted me to go so you can talk alone."

Jett chuckled at Rafe's oblivious behavior. "I didn't mean to interrupt everyone's meal."

"You didn't," Cindy said. "I've been wondering how you're doing."

"My back is doing a lot better these days. I should graduate from physical therapy soon. I'm still going to meetings," Jett said. "Getting close to a year now."

"That's awesome, dude." Rafe wiped his mouth.

"RJ is starting school soon. Delia's up in Four Bears today to do some clothes shopping for him."

"Four Bears has good stores?" Rafe said. "Since when?"

"Actually, there's a growing movement there to

revitalize the downtown," Cindy added about the town on the other side of Mercy Mountain. "If I ever get my second book done, I'm thinking of adding a day or two there each week for my practice."

"You're staying? You're not going back to Utah after your sabbatical?" Rafe asked.

"I'm strongly considering staying."

"What's your second book about?" Jett asked, trying to keep attention off Rafe, who accidentally dribbled blueberry into his beard. *Talk about a crush on Doc Cindy.*

"The physical and emotional progression of intimacy in relationships," Cindy answered matter of fact.

Rafe coughed, glancing at Jett with a fresh gleam in his eye, He swiped the napkin over his beard when he picked up on the signal Jett gave by tapping his own chin.

"How's married life treating you?" Rafe asked.

"Fine."

"Taking it slow?" Rafe stuffed another bite of pie in his mouth.

"What makes you say that? Have you been talking to Jim?"

"Nope." Rafe turned to Cindy. "I know you're the Doc here, but I have a sixth sense about these things. I know when someone's sneaking up on me from my Army days, *and* I know when people are getting la…uh…or not."

Cindy put a hand to her cheek and grinned Rafe's direction. "My, do you know who's been naughty and who's been nice too?"

"I just might," Rafe said with a shit-eating grin.

Jett raised an eyebrow. *Why Doc Cindy that was downright flirty with the big man Rafe.* "You two are funny together." He shook his head and chuckled. "I needed a laugh today."

When the waitress came by again, Cindy held out her salad bowl to be taken, then picked up Rafe's empty plate and handed it over too.

"Seriously, would you rather I shove off?" Rafe asked.

"No, stay."

Cindy leaned forward. "What's happening?"

"RJ's mom, Annie, is in Ashnee Valley. I met with her and the lady from Child Services yesterday. You both know Annie's not doing well, right?"

Cindy nodded. "I heard, but not any details."

"No," Rafe replied.

"She has liver disease. She's not a candidate for a transplant. It's terminal."

"Is that why she left RJ and took off?" Rafe asked.

"I'm sure it is. I think she's been scoring pain killers, but not in a legitimate way. Things are getting worse now. I don't have much information."

"Unless you're an emergency contact for Annie, no one can tell you much," Cindy said.

"That makes sense." Jett exhaled. "Delia suggested we get another cottage ready at the lodge and move Annie near us. We won't be renting rooms beyond the main lodge until sometime next spring."

"Whoa." Rafe sat back. "She decided that quick

after meeting her?"

"She hasn't even met her yet, which is something else I wanted to talk to you about, Doc."

"I imagine Delia's suggestion comes as a shock?" Cindy asked after a pause.

"Definitely." He scratched his ear. "To be honest, I was hoping Annie never showed up. I guess that sounds pretty cold."

"It seems a very human reaction to the situation," Cindy said. "You and Annie were never close. She kept RJ a secret from you for years."

"What are Delia's reasons for wanting to do this?" Rafe asked.

"She's looking at it from an emotional perspective on RJ's behalf. Plus, her mother passed away when she was a little girl. I don't know if she's thought about the reality of the situation."

Cindy nodded. "I assume Annie doesn't have insurance from what you've said. There's the care level required, and the cost."

"The family is going to take care of Annie's needs regardless."

"Wow," Cindy and Rafe said simultaneously.

"But go back a second." Rafe sat forward and tapped his finger on the table. "You said Delia's mom passed away when she was young. Was her mom sick also?"

"I was just wondering the same thing," said Cindy.

"Yes." Jett glanced from one to the other. "What?"

"Delia's doing it for them and herself," Rafe said.

"I'm impressed," Cindy agreed with a nod in Rafe's direction before looking back at Jett. "It's possible this is not only a way for RJ and his mother to be together. It could be a way for Delia to gain closure for herself too, essentially by creating this opportunity for your son."

"You got all that from what I said?" Jett asked.

"Sixth sense." Rafe tapped his temple.

"Twelve years of school and many years of experience," Cindy noted. "What do you want to do, Jett?"

He dropped his shoulders. "When Delia mentioned the idea of Annie living next door, I didn't like it. But I've seen Annie and thought about it more. I realize it's the right thing to do. I can't turn RJ's mother away if she's dying."

"You could talk to Kai and Leo about arranging someone from the clinic to help with her care, so it doesn't fall so much on you or Delia." Cindy said. "I'll be happy to see Annie too if she needs emotional support, no charge, of course. If I come by from time to time, you and I could pick up on regular conversations again also, if you like."

"Those are good ideas. I think I'll need every one of them."

"I can help," Rafe said. "I can take on more construction work whenever you need me to."

Overwhelmed, he lowered his chin. "Thank you."

"It won't be easy," Cindy said. "But the two of us and your family…we'll all be here. You're not alone. Did you want me there when Delia meets

Annie?"

"I want you there for that, and it would be the first time RJ sees her in months."

"I'd be happy to. I do have a suggestion and that's to have the meeting at my office."

"Neutral territory," Rafe said.

"Exactly. Plus, everyone all at once would be too hard on RJ. If you're open to it, maybe you'd let me meet with Annie and RJ first before you and Delia join us."

"If that's what you think is best, then yes."

"How soon?"

"Can we do it the day after tomorrow? I know it's a Saturday. I don't want to make Annie wait longer."

"Let's say ten a.m. I can spend an hour with RJ and his mother, then you and Delia could join us at eleven."

Jett nodded. "Thank you."

"You Mannis boys." Rafe put a hand on his shoulder. "God bless America. You somehow attract women with the biggest hearts to Ashnee Valley, but not without your fair share of drama."

# Chapter 9

THAT EVENING, JETT PULLED HIS truck to the side of Moon Ridge Road when his phone vibrated in his pocket.

"Quit peeking in the bucket," he told RJ, who kept tipping the round cover up a quarter inch and sticking his nose in for a sniff of the chicken for their dinner.

"Hello. Tell me you're close, woman." Jett chuckled. "That's the last time you leave town to shop all day."

"I got RJ some great clothes for the fall," Delia answered. "I take it you two missed me?"

"We'll show you how much when you get home. After dinner you can play with RJ. I've met my quota for board games." He reached over ruffling RJ's hair.

"I should be there in about fifteen minutes. How did your conversation with Doc Cindy go?"

"We're on for Saturday morning. We have tonight and tomorrow so we can explain it to…"

"I understand," Delia said.

"I told Jim I need tomorrow off. Let's spend

the day outdoors. We can do some hiking and fishing."

"Yay," RJ said.

Delia laughed into the phone. "That's a good idea. We can take our time and prepare RJ to see his mom."

"Right. In the meantime, I want to enjoy a regular night. I'm going to pull back on the road. Here's RJ, he wants to talk to you. See you in a few."

He handed the phone to his son and listened to the enthusiastic description of the afternoon from RJ's perspective.

Twenty minutes later, he turned off the main road and up the hill. His headlights shed a spotlight on Delia and five or six large shopping bags on the front porch. As soon as he pulled the truck to a stop, RJ unbuckled himself and jumped out.

Jett managed to walk, barely keeping himself from running toward her with the same eagerness, wondering what sense it really made to keep holding himself back.

"Don't panic," he said in her ear when she stood after giving RJ a hug.

"What do you mean?"

"You're it." RJ swatted Delia on the back of her leg.

"After supper, you're it." He picked up several of the clothing bags. "Hide and seek," he further explained. "You have no idea the fun you've missed." Jett tilted his head at her uneasy expression. "You, okay?"

"I haven't played hide and seek in a very long

time, that's all."

Jett put the last plate in the dishwasher, added soap and turned it on.

"Daddy." RJ walked into the kitchen and tugged his hand leading him to the guest bedroom. He stopped next to the side of the bed where Delia sat on the floor.

"You found her." He nudged RJ forward with a hand on his back. "Go on and tag her, you won."

"She's crying," RJ said.

"No, she isn't. Go on, now," he chuckled when his son dug his heels into the floor and wouldn't budge.

"We banded her." RJ peeked up at him. *Lord, it's cute when he talks in that little boy way.*

"Banded? You mean like a bird? No, she knows how you play hide and seek. She's just joshing you."

"A-banded. She says a-banded her."

He squatted in front of her. "Delia, are you crying?" Well, hell if his son wasn't right. A-banded?

*Abandoned. Oh boy.*

He took her hand and she gripped tight.

"Come here, buddy." He put his other hand on RJ's shoulder. "I'm going take care of Delia right now, so I need you to be a big boy and get yourself ready for bed. I'll come in and read you a story in a bit. Can you do that for me?"

RJ nodded and patted his little hand flat on top of Delia's head and bent to peek at her. "Don't cry. It's okay now. Daddy's going to take care of you."

Wiping her eyes, she smiled, and Jett could tell she was trying not to scare RJ.

"I'm just so tired, do you ever feel like that?" Delia asked in a shaky voice.

"Yes, ma'am."

He appreciated how Annie had taught RJ to speak to others respectfully. The boy was a master at please and thank you, yes sir and yes ma'am.

"Okay, little man, I want you to do three things, put on your pajamas, brush your teeth, and pick out a story, then get yourself in bed."

"That's four things."

"Very good. You're right. Can you remember all of them?"

RJ nodded.

"Then off you go. I'll be there in a few minutes." He watched his boy run out of the room, amazed something so small could imitate a herd of elephants.

He took another look at Delia's tear-stained face, then stood, pulling her up. He put an arm around her back, his other arm under her knees, and lifted her up.

"What are you doing?" she asked startled.

"Something I should have already." He had the decency to hold in a grunt as he shifted her weight in his arms. She was light, but the lift challenged his muscles. He carried her past RJ's room, down the hall to the master bedroom. He could hear the water running in the bathroom. He set her on the edge of the bed.

"Get undressed." He turned down the covers

and placed his hands on his hips. "Put on that prairie nightgown you're so fond of and wait for me."

"Gee, you gave RJ four things to do. I only get three?"

He grinned at her sass. "All right, here's another. Think about your husband holding you all night because that's what we'll be doing when I get back."

The soft click of the bedroom door closing was exactly twenty-seven minutes after he'd told her to wait for him. Not that he watched the clock. She had lit a candle on the bedtable that cast a soft glow in the room. Delia faced away from the door, but he could tell she wasn't asleep by the small shift under the covers.

Maybe he'd been a bit heavy-handed in the way he ordered her around. Walking toward the bed, he quickly unbuttoned his shirt, pulling it from his shoulders and tossing it on a chair next to the closet. He sat on the end of the bed and pulled off his boots.

"Do you want me on my stomach or back?" Delia asked.

He reached behind him and grabbed her ankle through the covers giving it a playful yank.

"Don't make me question my plan to cuddle you."

He pushed his jeans down, keeping his boxers on, then crawled in and pulled the sheet back over the two of them.

"Come here." Her eyes filled with tears, and he stopped her from turning away. "Delia, look at me."

"What are you going to do?"

"Damn girl, we're going to snuggle. And you're going to talk and I'm going to listen." He laughed softly. "Did you want me to say I was going to ravish you?"

"Maybe a little." She lay on her side looking at him. "I hate this. I hate that I'm afraid."

"Of me?"

"No." She sighed. "Myself."

"Why did hide and seek scare you tonight?"

Every muscle in her body tensed.

"I played it with my mother, and she would pass out. She'd forget we were even playing. I'd find her asleep after waiting for what felt like forever for her to find me."

He shifted close, his body an inch from hers, his hand on the small of her back. "I won't abandon you or RJ."

"When she was angry, she'd flaunt herself at other men in front of my father. I may have been a little girl, but I knew what she was doing. Sometimes it was a neighbor, or the mailman, even my teachers at school. I don't know if she was actually ever unfaithful, but she wanted him to believe she had been."

Pulling her close, he wrapped his arms around her and kissed her forehead. "I'm sorry. He brushed a single tear slipping down her cheek. "What else?"

"She died."

"Oh, honey." His fingers squeezed her hip as he spoke. "It's going to be okay. Trust me."

"I want to," she said lifting her gaze to his as she sat up. Putting both hands on his chest, she pushed so he was lying on his back. Lifting her leg, she straddled his body and lowered, hip to hip, chest to chest, her head buried in his neck.

"So, all this time, you just wanted to be on top?" He asked as he ran his hands along her back.

Her laughter sifted all her softness onto his hardness in the most appetizing way. He moved his hips in a lazy circle enjoying her soft moan in response. Lifting on her arms, she gazed at him, and he basked in her arousal, spell-bound, before her eyelids fluttered closed.

"Open your eyes, sweetheart." He rocked his hips, eager to see pure lust on her face again. "Delia, do you want me to help you feel good?"

On her tiny nod, he drew her nightgown slowly up the back of her legs and over her hips, cupping his big hands around her smooth bottom.

"No pantaloons. I appreciate that."

He slid her off his body and moved further down the bed.

He let out a woosh of breath as he pushed her legs apart. "Honeybee, every inch of you is perfect."

When his fingers brushed the downy hair of her sex, she sat up then flopped back covering her eyes with her hands.

"Should I stop?"

She shook her head and relaxed, letting her legs fall farther apart.

He separated her folds with his thumbs, circling her clit with his tongue before whipping his head back when she speared up on the bed again.

"This only works if you lie back."

Her eyes were closed as she spoke. "I've had sex with plenty of men..."

"Let me rephrase that," he growled. "This only works if you lie back and don't talk to me about other men."

"I don't really do this part...often."

His gaze lowered then lifted to her face. "Foreplay or oral?"

"Both. It's often just...boom."

*Those guys were jerks.* He prowled slowly up her body to kiss her lips. "No boom for now." He chuckled. "Lie back."

"Jett."

"Delia?"

"Please."

"Please what?"

"Please don't stop."

Her erotic invitation boosted his confidence. "Not a chance." He moved off the end of the bed. With his hands under her knees he pulled, bringing her to the edge.

"What are you doing?"

"Put your legs over my shoulders." He knelt, sliding his hands under her bottom lifting as he bent forward.

"I'm taking my fill." He placed small kisses along the delicate skin of her inner thighs. "Taking my sweet time." He blew cool air over her folds, smiling when her head fell back with a moan.

"All this pretty pink softness…" He glanced up to see her propped up again on her elbows watching his every move.

*I like that.*

Without touching her, he could see how wet her pussy lips were and tenderly slipped two fingers inside.

"Just for me," he said and leaned forward sucking her clit into his mouth as he curled his fingers.

"Oh my God." Delia moaned pushing her hips closer in his direction.

He lifted. "Good?"

"Yes." She slid her hands underneath her nightgown to touch her breasts.

*Lord, that is hot.*

He stroked his fingers as he sucked the tiny bundle of nerves and flittered his tongue. Soon, on a first tremble, the first tug around his fingers, he doubled his efforts wanting her pleasure. His cock swelled painfully as he imagined coming on her tits… her back… inside.

"Jett!"

Her inner walls milked his fingers as her knees shook. He stayed with her, eventually softening to tiny kisses until her hand touched the top of his head.

"That was the most incredible thing I've ever seen." He glanced at his lap, his penis sticking out of his boxer shorts. "I need a minute."

He stood and walked toward the bathroom.

"Wait, don't go."

He turned as Delia pushed her nightgown

down her legs and scooted back up on the bed, resting against the headboard.

"Stay."

He tilted his head to the side. "I'm only human, honey. That was…" he paused "…very sexy. I need to…"

She bit her lip. "You could show me."

*Damn.* He lowered his chin. "Yeah?"

Delia lifted a shoulder, a naughty smile tugging at the corner of her lips. "Seems fair."

He walked back and took off his boxer shorts next to the bed. He put a knee on the mattress. "Are you sure?"

At her nod, he settled on the bed, legs spread, his cock jutting up. Wrapping his hand around himself, he groaned as her eyes held his briefly.

She didn't make eye contact with him after that. Her gaze laser focused as he stroked along his shaft, squeezing at the top and sliding back down.

With a brazen whimper she touched a finger to her lips, and he dropped his head back, cresting more intensely than he could ever remember before.

Sometime during the night, she'd removed her nightgown and in the early morning, Jett pressed his chest to her back, pushed her hair away from her shoulder and snuggled his nose to her neck. When she arched, he slid his hand down her hip, lifting her top leg and pushing it forward.

"Delia." He groaned. "You aren't acting, are

you?"

She twisted with a look over her shoulder. "No. I wouldn't do that. I'm not pretending."

"Fuck." Jett rested his hand on her hip. "I don't have any condoms."

"I just started back on the pill," she said, pushing her soft bottom against him again.

He slid his hand down her stomach and circled her clit with his thumb. Edging closer, he entered slowly, one breathtaking inch at a time, until fully seated. He wanted to make her orgasm good again and kept his pace constant as his hands roamed between her breasts gently squeezing and tweaking her nipples.

"You feel good. I'm so close," Delia said.

She arched suddenly with a small cry, her muscles drawing him gloriously deep, and he pumped, fucking hard through the quivering shockwaves coursing along his cock as they peaked together.

Delia's phone vibrated when she reached the top of Dragonfly Hill on Friday afternoon. Behind her Jett, RJ, Kai, and four of Kai's five kids followed. She read a text from Sofia.

**Sofia:** What's the latest?

**Delia:** We're hiking Dragonfly Hill. Kai's clan is here too. No Leo or Will.

**Sofia:** Wish I was there. Jim has me photographing roofing material he's unhappy with so he can fire off irate emails to get a refund.

She chuckled at the eight emojis with various faces in pain or disgust then typed back.

**Delia:** Wish you were here too. It's four-thirty and we haven't told RJ about tomorrow. Jett keeps stalling. I think he's trying to wear RJ out first.

**Sofia:** Or himself. Can you imagine how he feels? He gets to be trapped in a room with his son's mother, his wife, and his therapist.

**Delia:** We slept together.

**Sofia:** When?

**Delia:** Last night.

**Sofia:** Holy crap. Dare I ask?

**Delia:** I'm in deep now.

**Sofia:** That's what he said.

Despite everything happening, Delia cracked up.

**Delia:** Gotta go. The gang has caught up.

**Sofia:** Call me later.

"What so funny?" Kai stopped next to her panting with Suze in her arms.

Delia waved her off. "Sofia. She sent a silly text." She tapped Suze's nose. "Did you make your poor mom carry you?"

"Sweaty mom." Kai said and handed Suze over. "You take her."

Delia hoisted Suze onto her hip. "Come on. Let's go look at your grandmother's artwork." She walked toward Catherine Kendall Mannis' sculpture, *Cammie's Delight*.

"Hey, sweet pea," Jett said as he came up next to them and gave Suze a kiss on her forehead. Turning to Delia, he said, "We're finally installing the rest of my mom's sculptures along the paths up at the lodge next week."

"I can't wait to see all of them there," she said.

"It's been a long time coming. For over twenty years, most of her artwork has sat in the basement of the lodge. We'll put in the signage that goes with each sculpture in the spring."

"I get teary-eyed thinking about it." Kai touched Jett's arm. "I'm so proud of you and Jim for all the work you're doing. Mom would be over-the-moon."

"Thanks Kai."

"Pick me up too." RJ said and Jett lifted him.

"Hopclopper." Suze pointed at the Dragonfly at Cammie's sculpted fingertip.

"That's a dragonfly." Kai's oldest daughter Jocelyn corrected. "She thinks it's a grasshopper."

"Somebody looks sleepy," Kai said with a head tilt toward RJ who rested on Jett's shoulder. She held out her arms to take Suze.

"We need to get going. I forgot snacks and Aiden and Luke are on the edge of a total meltdown. Plus, Suze has another evaluation tomorrow."

"We should get going too," said Delia.

Jett motioned everyone to go ahead of him as they started back down the hill. "What evaluation is this?"

Kai answered over her shoulder. "It's for an aide for school. Since she'll be mainstreamed, she's eligible. I'm also getting her on the bus with the other kids. She'll be riding with her sister and brothers and not on some separate bus."

"Is that a big deal?" Delia asked.

"You have no idea." Kai answered. "I'll get it done."

Jett chuckled from behind. "I don't doubt it. Do not mess with the Kai."

"Hopclopper." Suze repeated.

For all the plans to ease into telling RJ about seeing his mom, Jett didn't end up talking to him about it until early on Saturday morning.

"Let's not force it," Delia had suggested the night before when RJ started nodding off after an early supper and bath time. "He's too worn out."

She set a bowl of cereal in front of RJ at the kitchen table this morning and sat down.

"Do you want some breakfast?" she asked Jett.

"No, thanks."

"Coffee is plenty for me too."

Jett took a deep breath. "RJ, do you understand what I said earlier about seeing your mom today?"

RJ nodded. "Yes. I see Mommy and your friend."

"Right. After you see your mom, then Delia and I will be there too."

"Okay. Will I go home with Mommy?"

Delia glanced at the tightening muscles of Jett's jaw. "Today is just a visit," she said, jumping in. "You'll come home here and then see your mom again on another day."

"Where will Mommy go?"

Jett glanced at Delia. "We're going to help your mom get settled nearby so she can see you."

She pushed her chair back and walked to the

sink, pouring the rest of her coffee down the drain. "I'll shower and get ready to go."

"Can I watch cartoons?" RJ asked.

She stopped in the hallway and put a hand to her chest.

*It's going to be okay.*

An hour and a half later, Jett opened the downtown door to Doc Cindy's office and gestured for Delia and RJ to go up the stairs first. Her office sat above the Queen Bee Bookstore on Main Street. In the early days of his sobriety, Cindy counseled him for free. She'd even babysat for RJ the night of his accident.

"RJ," Annie said when Delia opened the door to the lobby. "Look at you, you're so big."

Jett stepped around Delia and put his hand on RJ's back. "It's okay buddy. Take your time."

"Mommy?"

Annie got on her knees and RJ went right to her open arms. "Yes, sweetie. I've missed you."

Jett turned, his back to the reunion. He put his hand on Delia's elbow and drew her farther into the room.

"Good morning, everybody," Cindy Wheeler said, walking into the lobby with an easy smile. "I don't think we've all met." She put her hand out. "Hi Delia, I'm Cindy. Annie, this is Delia Kincaid, Jett's wife."

Delia shook Dr. Wheeler's hand and faced Annie. "Good morning. It's good to meet you."

Annie stood, holding RJ's hand. "Nice to meet

you too."

Cindy approached RJ and squatted to his level. "Hi, RJ. Do you remember me? I'm Cindy. I'm looking forward to spending some time with you today along with your mom and dad and Delia."

RJ shrunk back leaning against Annie's leg.

"It's okay." Jett repeated. "Remember what we talked about. You're going to visit with your mom and Cindy. And we'll be back in a little bit to join you."

RJ nodded.

"RJ, would you like to see the aquarium I have in my office?" Cindy asked. "I have many fish. Maybe now would be a good time for your mom to show you."

Jett kept an eye on Annie and RJ as they walked down the hallway to Cindy's office.

"God dammit," he muttered when they were out of earshot.

"I know this is really tough. There's a lot of trust needed today. You're doing fine."

"Is an hour enough time before we come back?" Delia asked.

"We're coming back in a fucking hour." Jett flung open the door to the stairs. "Not one minute more."

His outburst didn't faze Doc Cindy. "An hour is perfect. We'll see you then."

They reached the bottom of the steps and stood outside. "Fuck," Jett said.

"I think my heart was just torn from my chest," Delia added quietly.

"Let's walk." He took her hand. "We can go to

the park. I don't feel like being on the street and having to talk to anyone."

When they reached city park, he found a bench near the water for them to sit.

"What are we doing after?" she asked.

Jett shrugged. "RJ will need lunch. I was hoping to go to a meeting at one o'clock."

"What did Cindy mean when she said a lot of trust is needed today? Does she mean trusting each other or trusting the process?"

"Trusting the process, I imagine. How could anyone trust Annie?"

Delia leaned her head to the side. "I don't know. But she is RJ's mother. She doesn't look well at all. I feel bad for her."

Jett rubbed his chin with his thumb. "I trust you."

She scooted close and rested her head on his shoulder. "I trust you too." She glanced up. "We're a team."

"Are you okay with what happened between us the other night?"

She lifted his arm and put it around her shoulder and rested her head again. "Yes." She put her arm around his middle and hugged.

"We're good together." He stroked his fingers gently through her hair.

"We are." She sat up. "If I still want to go slow in the sex department, can we do that?"

"Yeah, we can do that. You lead. I'll follow." He kissed her forehead.

"Thank you. Okay, how many more minutes do we have left now?"

"Forty."

She dropped her forehead against his chest, her groan muffled in his shirt.

A short time later, Delia fidgeted in her seat next to Jett on a couch in Doc Cindy's office. Across from them, RJ sat on Annie's lap. Tension seeped off Jett as he kept glancing at the clock on the wall.

"It's almost noon and we need to get lunch. I have a meeting at one o'clock." Jett stood and motioned to RJ. "Come on buddy. Time to go."

RJ clung to Annie. "I don't want to go."

"Time to go," Jett said.

RJ put his shoulders back and frowned. "No."

Delia sat forward on the edge of the couch. Annie rubbed RJ's back but didn't encourage anything productive. She glanced to Doc Cindy, calm as ever.

"Do we have more options we could consider?" Cindy asked.

Jett sighed. "It's been two hours. That's enough. Let's decide on another day and time."

"Tomorrow," Annie said.

"I work tomorrow," said Jett.

"You don't have to be here. You can send your wife to watch me."

Delia fixed Annie with a piercing look. *You're making it hard to like you, lady.*

"How about I go get everyone lunch," Delia suggested after a pause. "Jett can go to his meeting. RJ can spend some more time here."

"I'll leave before you get back from your meeting, okay?" Annie added. "That will make this easier."

RJ pouted. "I don't want you to go."

"Mommy has some things to do later this afternoon. We can have another visit soon, okay?"

"Would that work for you, Jett?" Cindy asked.

A tiny muscle twitched under his left eye when he looked at Delia. "What will you do while I'm at my meeting?"

"I can sit in the lobby or go to the bookstore."

"All right. I'll go with you to get the food."

"Actually…" Cindy said, "I was hoping I could speak with you for a few minutes alone, Jett."

Delia stood and picked up her purse. "You stay. I'll get sandwiches and drinks."

*Right after I run myself into a brick wall.*

Doc Cindy opened her office door. "We have a plan. Annie and RJ, help yourself to bottled waters in the small fridge if you're thirsty. I'll rejoin you in a few minutes."

"Okay," Annie said with a quick glance at Delia. "Thank you."

She mustered a curt nod and led the way out of the room, Jett and Doc Cindy following. "I'll be back with lunch."

"What the ever-loving fuck, Doc?" Jett said. "Is this what this is going to be like from now on? RJ pouts and Annie runs the show?"

Cindy gestured for them to move to the far side of the lobby and sit.

"Take a breath. You knew today would be hard."

"Not this hard." Jett paced.

"One hour at a time. It's good you planned ahead to go to a meeting. Believe it or not, you and Delia are handling this better than a lot of people would. It's not the time to push."

"Delia's out there," he swung his arm toward the window, "like she's some errand girl to this drama."

"If you didn't notice, she needed a break too. There are going to be moments like this when you'll have to give each other space."

Jett rubbed his temples at the massive headache coming on. *Food will help.* He sat in one of the armchairs.

"What did you want to talk to me about?"

Cindy took a seat.

"Unfortunately, Annie is further along in the progression of her disease than I realized. She gave permission for her doctor to share her medical records with me." Cindy paused. "This is not going to be a lingering illness."

"How long would you say she has?"

"A couple months at most. She fell in my office while you and Delia were gone. It was a stumble, and she's okay. Balance is an obvious issue." Cindy put her hands on her knees. "She's staying with a friend, but that's not going to be an option after a few more days."

"I can't get one of the other cottages ready for her that fast. I'd need…" He stopped to consider. "Two weeks and that would be pushing it."

Cindy sighed. "Jett, she can't be alone, even next

door to you. We're going to need to find a care facility for her or go with another alternative."

He dropped his chin. "Like what? Living in my house?"

"I realize that would be very different and something you and Delia would need to discuss. It is an option. As a practical matter, you'd be able to monitor RJ's time with her, including what he sees and doesn't see."

"This is the payback I get for being a complete asshole half my life."

Cindy shot him a frustrated glare. "I'm not saying this as your therapist, but as a friend who has known you a long time. That's horseshit and you know better."

*Fuck.* He cringed at the first sign of stress he'd noticed from Cindy.

"You're right," he said and sat up straight. "This isn't about feeling sorry for myself."

Hearing footsteps on the stairs, Jett got up and opened the door.

"Hi," he said to Delia and took one of the bags she carried. She set the other bag on the coffee table and glanced between them.

"Is there something you want me to know before we eat?"

Jett raked his fingers through his hair. "We need to talk about having Annie move in with us and not next door."

"I see." Delia unloaded sandwiches from the bags. "Let's do it."

"You're okay with that idea?" He dipped his chin. "We could speak with Leo and Kai first and get some advice on it."

"I don't think that's necessary for making the decision. Let's offer it to Annie and figure out the rest as we go." She put her hands on her hips. "I forgot drinks."

"I have plenty of waters," Cindy said.

Delia's movements were stiff and robotic as she organized the sandwiches and held out three of them to Doc Cindy.

"These are for RJ, Annie, and you."

"I'll eat out here with you and then get going to my meeting," Jett said.

"The two of you—" Cindy began.

"Don't." Delia shook her head. "Just…don't."

"Understood," Cindy said with a nod. "I'll grab those waters for you."

"Thanks." Jett turned to Delia once Cindy left the lobby. "This is a fucking disaster. I'm sorry."

Delia sighed. "It's not. And you don't need to be sorry. It's what we agreed to. It will be what's best for RJ."

She unwrapped her sandwich and took a bite. "Now, if you'll excuse me, I'm going to stuff this entire sandwich into my face and then go downstairs and eat pastries at the bookstore coffee shop for the next hour while you're at your meeting."

He laughed and rubbed the heel of his hand along his forehead. "Only you could make me laugh right now, Honeybee."

# Chapter 10

FOUR DAYS LATER, DELIA FILLED a glass with water and set it down in front of Annie at the cottage. She scanned the other woman's feathery, light brown hair with fading highlights. She could see the attraction Jett would have found in Annie's heart-shaped face with high cheekbones and jade green eyes.

"Where are you from originally?"

"Chicago," Annie answered.

"Perfect, one city girl to another. I grew up in New York. Jett and RJ should be here in a little bit." Delia took a long sip from her water bottle. "Jett doesn't seem to remember much about your time together."

"Time together?" Annie laughed and cupped her ample breasts.

Delia flinched at the crude gesture, working hard to keep her expression neutral.

"He saw these and said he had to have them. We went to his place. Fucked. I left. Two months later I found out I was pregnant."

"How charming."

"Too styled for you, New York?"

"No style sounds more like it." Hearing the graphic retelling of RJ's conception disappointed her — an event devoid of love or passion and barely coherent by all parties involved.

Annie tipped her head to the side and raised her glass. "That's my story. What's yours?"

It hadn't occurred to Delia she had a story and certainly if she did, not one she wished to share. All along, she'd made Annie the bad guy when the woman was nowhere to be found, doing God knows what. Delia convinced herself Jett may have somehow been seduced. Against his will.

*Hmm. She's right, I do have a story.*

Delia crossed her arms. "I'll level with you."

"Since I'm living in your house until I die, do we really have time for anything else?"

"No, we don't," Delia agreed. "My story, if you want to call it that, is I'll do anything to protect RJ. Don't doubt I'll protect him, even from you if needed, and regardless of the fact you're sick."

An awkward silence stretched between them.

"He's, *my* son."

"And Jett's."

"Do you love RJ?"

Delia uncrossed her arms, her hands clasped on the table in front of her. "I've never fallen so quickly. Yes, I love RJ. I want to help take care of him."

"When I'm dead."

"No, right now and I've started putting some money aside to invest in RJ's future."

Annie scoffed. "I could tell you came from money, must be nice."

"I grew up on Staten Island. My father is a retired cop. I don't come from money." Delia straightened her spine and swallowed the urge to share that her mother died an addict.

*Thank you very much.*

"I know how to work hard. I know how to earn money. In fact, I already have. I can make sure RJ has what he needs."

Annie squinted, studying her. "So, you're successful and good-looking. Now you want to take me in, a dying woman, and raise my son. Interesting."

More rattled than she dared let on, Delia peeled at the label on her water bottle.

"Dying makes a person see things for what they are. You definitely have a story."

Delia stood and poured the rest of her water in the sink before tossing the bottle in the recycle bin and turning toward Annie.

"There are house rules." She ignored the knowing nod Annie directed her way.

"Lay 'em on me."

"No alcohol. No drugs. One drop, one snort, you're out."

"First, I'm sober now. Second, I've never snorted anything in my life." Annie bowed her head. "I need pain pills. I'm not some low-life."

Delia sat down again. "I made some assumptions. I'm sorry. If you're taking pain medication, Kai or Leo will administer it."

"Who are they?"

"Jett's sister and her husband. They run the clinic in town. Doc Cindy has also offered to come by anytime you want to talk."

"Anything else?"

"You and Jett are RJ's parents. While you're staying here, I'll support you both. Maybe we won't ever like each other. But I respect you. You're his mother."

Annie's hand shook as she lowered her glass and tears spilled down her cheeks. "I didn't expect you to say something like that."

Delia came around the table to sit in the chair next to Annie and put her arm around the other woman's back.

"You're going to be with your son." For emphasis, she squeezed her hand on Annie's arm and made eye contact. "That way, RJ will remember your love all his life. That's what's important."

Jett stopped in the doorway, looking on as Delia reached for a napkin and handed it to Annie. Why did his mistakes become a burden to everyone? He couldn't stand either woman going through this. He loved RJ more than anything. He'd die for him. Yet, his past actions brought nothing but struggle. He squeezed RJ's hand to reassure him.

"Go to your mom, she needs a hug," he said, effectively announcing their arrival.

The hurt Delia couldn't hide strained her face as RJ crawled onto Annie's lap and wrapped his little arms around her neck.

"Come here," Jett said, holding out his hand

and leading her from the room.

He walked them through the house and out the sliding glass door to the patio. Sitting down, he pulled her gently onto his lap and wrapped his arms around her. It was a long time before he spoke.

"This situation is too much." He hugged her when she shook her head. "It's too much," he repeated, his voice husky with emotion.

Clearing his throat, he held her for a long time, then helped her off his lap and stood, cupping her cheeks with his hands.

"I'll always take good care of RJ. I won't fail him." The ache in his chest made his breathing shallow. "This should all be my burden, not yours. I know we talked about a year, but I'd never force anything on you."

He placed a tender kiss on her forehead and walked to the sliding door again.

"Where are you going?" she asked.

"I'll take Annie and RJ to Patsy's Diner for an early supper. Sofia is on her way. She called when we were coming up to the house. You two can have some time together. Let's just get Annie settled for now. We can talk about plans going forward later."

"There's nothing to talk about." Delia lifted her chin. "You keep forgetting this was my idea and by the way, I'm not fragile."

The next morning, Jett rose early, not wanting RJ or Annie to ask him why he'd slept on the couch. He put a hand on top of a pile of shingles and let the nail gun drop at his side. He'd been up since early dawn, climbing the ladder to the roof on one of the cottages farthest from his own and nailing the hell out of every shingle he could.

"Are you okay up there?"

He glanced down to find Annie asking the question.

"Should you be out here?" he snapped.

"Would you like some breakfast?"

"You made breakfast?"

She cocked her hip to the side and put one hand up to cover her eyes from the sun.

"Delia and RJ made pancakes. I offered to come find you. Are you coming?"

Jett backed down the ladder. He threw his gloves on the ground and pulled the bottom of his t-shirt up and wiped his forehead with it.

"Delia's not here to serve you."

"I know that. She has her hands full already."

Jett picked up his gloves and smacked them against his thigh. "You can see RJ as much as you want," he said as he walked away from her. "We'll make sure you're comfortable."

"Gee, thanks."

He stopped and turned back at her sarcasm. "What do you want from me?"

"Not a damn thing," she snapped back.

"Good answer."

"Fine. Your wife and son are waiting for you."

She brushed past, bumping his arm as she went, and headed up the sloping path. He followed, watching her stumble halfway up the hill. When she swayed, he ran forward catching her from behind.

"Don't touch me," Annie said, pulling away.

He let her go, staying near enough to steady her again if needed.

"Annie." He put his hands on his hips and looked at the ground. "I'm sorry," he said, making eye contact again. "I know this is hard on you too."

She stared at him with a look of agony on her face. "Do you think I want any of this? To live with strangers? To die?"

"No." He answered. "Of course not."

"Help me up this hill."

He offered his arm and walked slowly, realizing the progress he'd made now that someone leaned on him instead of the other way around.

"I have to ask you something," he said.

"What?"

He swallowed the lump in his throat. "Why did you keep RJ from me?"

"You can guess why."

"It's hard not to be mad about all I've missed."
*It hurts.*

"I stopped drinking for a long time." Annie said with more kindness to her tone. "Even though I left Colorado, I still had friends here. I knew you hadn't stopped. I didn't think RJ should be around you. Besides, I could barely handle myself."

She paused when they reached the top of the hill, her breath ragged.

"You should know he never went without. Sometimes it was a struggle, but he always had food and he's been safe. I kept him with me. I didn't leave him with anyone, ever. I did the best I could."

"I understand," Jett said. "Did you start drinking again because you were in pain?"

"Yes. I didn't know I was sick. Not like this. I hurt all the time. For a while I got by with booze and weed. Later I got clever enough to get my hands on prescription medicines, but not by going to a doctor. It's not enough."

"RJ told me he's seen someone hit you." He tilted his head to make sure he could determine truth or deceit from her eyes. "Is there anyone I need to be concerned about?"

She shook her head. "There's nobody. RJ is all I have."

A comfortable routine developed more easily than Delia expected in the early days after Annie moved in. Beyond the awkward first day, the two women managed to avoid territorial sparring.

In the mornings, Annie prepared RJ's breakfast, then played with him for another hour while Delia and Jett got ready for the day. Then she'd reappear in the evening when they ate dinner together. The three adults had taken to alternating nights putting RJ to bed and reading him a story.

Out of sight from RJ, staff from the clinic, often Leo or Kai, made a short visit each afternoon. Doc Cindy had been by twice so far.

Delia stood in the hallway this morning, eavesdropping on Jett and Annie talking in the kitchen.

"What are you doing?" Jett asked.

"I'm practicing making lunch for RJ. When he starts kindergarten tomorrow, I want to be the one that prepares it."

"That's nice. Are those brownies you made too?"

Delia rolled her eyes. Annie had a sweet tooth. If Jett wasn't working ten hours a day on the buildout of the property, she'd worry about the cupcakes and pie he scarfed down after dinner each night before crashing into bed.

"Here, do you want this sandwich for your lunch today? I made plenty of brownies. Help yourself."

"Thank you. I usually make my own lunch. Do my own laundry. I try to keep up with my own chores."

Delia bit her lip to avoid laughing.

"That sets a very good example for RJ," Annie said. "Okay, well, have a good day at work."

At that, Delia tip-toed back to the bathroom and shut the door. Stepping on the scale, she vowed to not overindulge in Annie's baking.

*Two pounds? I'm not even eating the cupcakes and cookies. Okay, maybe one cupcake. Yeah, but you're not rehearsing nine hours a day either.*

As she walked into the living room, she could hear Jett's truck starting up and the crunch of gravel under tires.

"You just missed him." Annie said, turning to look at her over the back of the couch.

"I'll see him at dinner."

"You are an interesting couple. Not even a kiss goodbye."

"I overheard the two of you talking in the kitchen," she said to change the subject as she settled in the armchair kitty-corner to the couch. "I didn't mean to listen in," she fibbed.

Annie chuckled. "They need a lot of praise, don't they?"

"Men? Yes."

"I do my own laundry." Annie imitated Jett's deep voice.

Delia smiled. "You were very generous with your response. What's RJ up to?"

"He's in his room packing his backpack. He's pretty excited for school tomorrow."

"It's a special day." Delia smiled. "I'm so glad you can go with Kai to take him. I have a doctor appointment tomorrow morning, and Jett has to be in Four Bears early, something for the lodge."

"I know what you're doing."

"Hmm?" Delia answered her eyes wide.

"Okay, we'll play it your way." Annie gave her a knowing look. "Thank you."

"I don't know what you're thanking me for. We should be thanking you."

Annie laughed outright. "That is some pathetic acting right there." She scrunched her nose. "People used to pay you for that?"

Delia sat forward, patting her hand to Annie's knee before standing. "I'm getting myself some coffee. I'll bring you your tea."

## Chapter 11

FROM HER KITCHEN WINDOW, DELIA could just make out the giant American flag flapping in the October breeze at the Little Forest Fairgrounds. Her hands warmed around a mug of coffee as she listened to the wind whip the awning over the back door. It was six weeks since Annie's arrival. The autumn weather promised another high wind day for Ashnee Valley.

The sound of Annie's cough from the back bedroom broke her melancholy, and she pushed back her chair to turn on the stove for the teakettle. Stopping at the bathroom, she ran hot water to fill the tub. At the bedroom door, Delia knocked and peeked in.

"How are you doing today?"

Annie rolled to face her. "Not good."

"I started a bath and some tea."

"Thank you."

Annie's cough kicked in again as Delia moved into the room to prop pillows, lifting, and adjusting the less than one-hundred-pound woman into a sitting position. Interrupted by the whistle on the stove, Delia left momentarily, returning with a teacup and crackers on a small tray she placed on the bedtable.

"How was RJ this morning?" Annie asked. "I heard him come in my room but couldn't get my eyes open to see him off."

"Happy as a clam. He has a huge crush on his kindergarten teacher, Miss Jenny." She handed the teacup to Annie.

"She's a cute one. She seems so young to me."

"Jenny is young." Delia chuckled. "She adores him. It's very sweet."

Annie took a sip, then handed the teacup to Delia before pushing herself down in the bed and pulling the covers up to her chin."

"How's Jett?"

"Fine," Delia said as she straightened the bed covers.

"Off to work already?"

"You know the routine. He leaves at the crack of dawn and returns at the crack of midnight. Well, practically. If he isn't at work, he's at a meeting or lifting weights now that he can."

Delia reigned in the sarcasm to her voice and quit fussing with the blanket. "Sorry, I know he and the others are working hard to get the lodge ready. Jim and Sofia are preparing for guests for Christmas and New Year's."

"I'm not going to make it to Thanksgiving, let alone all that."

"Stop," Delia offered in objection.

Annie put her hand up. "It's true."

"Let me check the tub. I'll be right back."

She returned a few minutes later and helped Annie sit. "Come on, I added bubbles this time. The hot water is going to feel good."

Kneeling next to the tub she rinsed shampoo from Annie's hair, then applied conditioner.

"Keep your eyes closed." Gentling her fingers, she massaged Annie's scalp. "Ugh, that smell." Delia gagged. "Sorry, I had no idea this bubble bath reeks."

"It smells lovely to me," Annie said. "I like it."

"Blech." Delia coughed.

Annie glanced at her. "Are you having an allergic reaction? Your eyes are all red. Are you crying?"

"No." Delia waved a hand in front of her. "It smells like my mother's perfume…" *And booze.* She tried to shake off nausea and the creeping edges of a panic attack. "It reminds me of her. God, she hated me."

"What are you talking about?"

It was not her voice, but haughty and familiar as she imitated her mother.

*'Just remember Delia, you're not as smart and pretty as you think. All you'll ever amount to is being a stupid little slut.'*

Annie gave her a wide-eyed look. "Your mom said that? How old were you?"

Delia cleared her throat. "Does it matter? Young. It was a long time ago. I'm sorry. Ancient history. I…ugh, this smell. It took me right back."

"Mmm, hmm. I see." Annie tilted her head to the side. "Was she physically abusive too?"

"No. Maybe a slap here or there. She was mean when she drank." Delia poured warm water to rinse Annie's hair.

"A slap here or there *is* abusive. Have you told anyone this before?"

"My dad knows, of course. I've told Jett a little."

"You haven't told Sofia?"

Delia scoffed. "About my mom calling me a slut, no."

"Sounds like she hates herself and you remind her of that. That's not anyone's responsibility but her own," Annie said.

She shrugged. "I hated her at times."

"That's not a surprise."

Delia wrapped a towel around Annie's head. "I'm sure some people would say I should forgive her. What do you think?"

"Me? Preach forgiveness? I don't have any credibility there. But I know you can hand over what was never yours to carry. You know what I'm saying? Look at yourself. You are an accomplished woman with a fancy career, a husband, and RJ. Somehow you got stuck washing my sorry ass in this tub, so your life is not perfect. Besides, what people? Fuck. That. Shit."

She laughed at the drawn-out way Annie said the last three words. "It doesn't matter. My mother is no longer alive."

"It does matter," Annie said, grabbing her hand and giving it a squeeze. "Your little girl self is asking you to set things straight right now in the present. Go on. You say it. Fuck that shit."

Straightening her shoulders, Delia inhaled

deeply.

Annie rolled her eyes. "Just say it."

"Fuck that shit."

"One more time with a little more gusto."

"Fuck. That. Shit. Lady," she said with more determination.

"There you go. Feel better?"

"Yes, actually." Delia helped Annie stand and handed her a towel to dry off. "That helped. Thank you."

"You're welcome. See how much more direct things can be when there isn't much time left?"

Annie patted the mattress next to her after Delia helped her back to bed.

"Sit with me. I've been wondering what's going on between you and Jett." Annie gripped her hand when she hesitated. "Don't run off, we're sharing our feelings today. You and Jett have been very good to me. I've been able to spend so much time with RJ. I can never thank you both enough. Especially you for what you've done for me as a mother. But I can see you two are struggling. Something happened right when I moved in, didn't it?"

Delia hung her head and squeezed Annie's hand.

"Oh, Annie. It wasn't your fault. We had shaky footing. Everything just got messed up."

"Come on, tell me." Annie patted the mattress again. "Maybe I can help with this too."

Delia sighed and lay down on the bed, staring at the ceiling.

"Will you pull the afghan over us?" Annie asked.

Delia sat up. "Are you cold? Do you want the heating pad by your feet?"

"No. I'm nosey. Tell me what that man's done to you." A coughing fit ripped through her again. It took several sips of tea to subside. "Shit, this is getting old."

Delia pulled the blanket over the two of them, plumped her pillow and settled with her arms above her head.

"Who would have seen us becoming friends, huh?"

"I know." Annie nodded. "We're gossipy girlfriends, just like you and Sofia. We're more than girlfriends, you bathe me. So, tell me why I'm not hearing the bed bumping up against my wall every night and why you and Jett act like brother and sister. That is, when you aren't smiling those pretend smiles for RJ's benefit. Turn with me and rub my back and spill it."

Delia scooted onto her side making small circles on Annie's back with the heel of her hand, the same way she'd seen Leo or Kai do when either one came to administer Annie's medications.

"We're just going through the motions." Delia kept rubbing as she spoke. "We haven't…we don't."

"What?" Annie turned, staring back at her, her mouth taking a perfect O-shape. "In all the time I've been here? Nothing?"

She pursed her lips. "Barely a kiss."

"Delia?" Jett's voice carried through the house and the back door slammed. "Where are you?"

"What's he doing home so soon?" Delia whispered.

"Why are we whispering?"

With a quick knock, Jett opened the door to the bedroom, took in the view of them spooning and slammed the door shut again.

"Sorry," he muttered from the hallway.

Annie burst out laughing. "Go on," she said with a nudge, her cough starting up again. "I need to rest. I don't feel right today."

Delia slipped off the bed and walked to the door. "Annie Reed, you are so much smarter than you let people think."

"I know. We'll figure out what to do later about this kissing problem."

Jett lowered the milk carton and wiped his mouth with the back of his hand. His overalls hung at his waist, his white, long sleeve undershirt hugging his chest still moist with sweat. Jim had called it a day, sending the crew home due to the wind once they got the tarps over the areas of the new cottage roofs that were still unfinished.

The main lodge was done now and most of the cottages would soon be finished. At least the exteriors. Inside, there were mechanicals to install, painting and decorating.

He turned, shaking an empty carton at Delia when she came into the kitchen.

"I'll have a bite to eat and then stop at the store for some milk. You can let me know if you need anything else."

She nodded at him. "You're home early."

"The winds are too high for roof work."

Looking at the dark circles under Delia's eyes, he regretted how awkward things had become between them. Other than sleeping at night, it was a rare event to find them in the same room together, let alone having a conversation. He discreetly gave her a once over. She wore white yoga pants and a gray sweatshirt, her hair in a ponytail, a far cry from the stylish New Yorker she'd once been.

After they made it through the holidays and rounded into spring, the year would nearly be up. The marriage would have served its purpose. It sure as hell wasn't serving any purpose to either him or Delia now. Although he had to admit it had been the best arrangement for RJ and that was his goal.

He stepped out of the way as she reached around him for her cell phone on the kitchen counter and dialed.

"Kai, hi, it's Delia. Um, Annie seems much worse today."

Jett leaned his hip on the counter, crossing his arms and listening.

"She's coughing all the time, and she says she doesn't feel right."

Delia listened, holding the phone to her ear, looking down at the floor and then out the kitchen window.

"Yes, there's a raspy sound, a wheezing to it."

Jett pushed off the counter and stood behind her his hand on her shoulder, his head bent so he could hear too.

"Put her on speaker," he said. "Kai, its Jett. I just got home. What are you saying?"

"It doesn't sound good to me. Has Annie mentioned increased pain, Delia?"

"No, she hasn't."

"Jett? "Kai said. "Would you go take a listen to her breathing? Delia, you and Jett will need to start preparing RJ when he gets home today. The way we talked about. Do you understand?"

"No. Oh God, Kai. The bus is going to be here any minute."

Jett returned, glancing at panic creeping across Delia's face. He shook his head.

"She's asleep, but her breathing doesn't sound good," he told Kai.

"Leo's getting ready to head over. He'll be there soon. Let's keep her comfortable. We're probably looking at a matter of days now."

Jett gently took the phone from Delia's hand.

"Thanks, Kai." He set the phone on the counter, standing with his front to Delia's back, his body almost touching. When she turned, burrowing herself in his chest, he held tight, rubbing her back.

"The bus is here," he said and stepped back. "I'll go. It's going to be better if RJ sees her as much as possible today even if she's sleeping. Later will be too difficult."

He kissed Delia's forehead then grabbed his coat off the back of the kitchen chair and went outside.

# Chapter 12

SEVENTY-TWO HOURS LATER, HIS FAMILY had been to visit and already left again. Kai brought meals, most of the food still sitting untouched in the refrigerator.

Sofia and Jim went back home after giving RJ a bath and reading to him until he fell asleep.

Leo planned to stay the night. Doc Cindy came by too, spending an hour alone with Annie who was no longer conscious.

And Delia walked outside in the cold, traveling along the path leading from the back patio to the woods over and over. Jett stepped out occasionally to get some air and check on her.

"She's fine," his father said from his chair next to the sliding glass door. "I'm keeping an eye on her. Everyone handles this sort of thing in their own way."

At one in the morning, Leo stepped out of Annie's room and motioned to Jett.

"I think you should go in."

"Son," Ben said, surprising Jett who thought

his dad had fallen asleep, "let her know RJ is safe, so she can go in peace."

Jett stepped into the room, dimly lit with a soft glow from a nightlight. Leo moved to the bed, checking her pulse before tucking her covers again.

"She's not in any pain," he said and gathered some supplies and his sweater off the back of the chair. He opened the door to the bedroom. "There's no wrong way, do whatever feels natural."

Annie lay on her side. Jett pulled a chair next to the bed and sat, resting his hand on her upper arm.

"I'm here. Everything is going to be okay. RJ is asleep." He smiled at her even though her eyes were closed. "You're a good mother."

He sat back holding one of her hands. After a long while, he sat forward as her breathing became noticeably shallow and brushed her hair from her forehead.

"RJ loves you very much, Annie. Thank you for our son."

It shocked him how fast the room fell silent when Annie's breath hitched and suddenly stopped.

Leo and Ben stood as he made his way back into the dark living room.

"She's gone."

Leo nodded, a hand to Jett's shoulder. His cell phone illuminated the hallway as he headed toward the bedroom. "I'll make some calls."

"Dad," Jett whispered. "It's late. You should take

the spare bed in RJ's room and get some sleep."

"I'll wait until Sheriff Tanner and the others arrive, then I'll take you up on that."

"I'm going to go talk to Delia," Jett said and went outside.

Less than twenty minutes later the sheriff had arrived. Jett tried to get Delia to stay out of the living room as Annie's body was brought outdoors to the waiting vehicle, but she refused. Thankfully, RJ slept through it all. It would be difficult enough to tell him in the morning that his mother had died.

He stood in the driveway, his breath visible in the cold air as he spoke with the man from the funeral home and shook the sheriff's hand. Out of the corner of his eye he caught a glimpse of Delia walking quickly toward his truck. She started the engine and drove off, gravel crunching beneath the tires.

"Excuse me, Sheriff," Jett said as he jogged quickly toward the house. He searched RJ's room first before knocking on the bathroom door.

"Dad, where's Delia going? She just left in my truck."

"I have no idea. You best go after her. You can take mine. The keys are in my coat pocket."

He fumbled through his father's jacket and ran out the front door, just in time to catch a glimpse of the police car's taillights as the sheriff made a left out of the lodge.

*Where is she going? Think.*

Ten minutes later he spotted headlights as he drove past the Little Forest Fairgrounds. He found her, parked in the middle of the field, facing the trees, motor running. He pulled up next to her and jumped from his vehicle, ran to the driver side and pulled the door open. Delia's head rested on the steering wheel, her shoulders shaking.

"Oh, Honeybee, scoot over." He tapped her thigh and she slid to the right as he climbed into the truck and shut the door. "Come here."

He put his arm around her and tucked her close.

"Jesus, you scared the hell out of me. Are you okay?" He brushed her hair out of her face and examined her. "Answer me, baby."

"It's not a panic attack," she took several deep breaths, then opened the glove box for a tissue and blew her nose.

He rubbed her back then switched to massaging the base of her skull, trying to ease tension.

"What can I do?"

"I'm okay." She sniffled. "Thanks for coming to find me. I just can't believe she's gone. Three days ago, we were laughing together. She was going to help me with a problem."

Jett tucked her hair behind her ear. "What problem was that?"

"Figuring out why you stopped wanting to be near me. Why you stopped kissing me months ago."

"I've never stopped wanting to be near you." He let out a breath. "The last thing I wanted to be is another person you felt obligated to take care of. Come on, it's late. Tomorrow is already here. It's going to be a tough day for RJ."

"I've missed you." She snuggled close, her soft breath flittering over the sensitive skin behind his ear. He reacted with a groan that ratcheted the air to crackling anticipation.

"I've missed you too." He rubbed a hand over his face and sighed. "My dad is at the house..."

"We can be quiet."

The gentle kiss he bestowed quickly became desperate between them.

He pulled away, studying the restless longing in Delia's eyes. "Are you sure about this?"

"Yes. Please. Can't we face reality tomorrow instead?"

He didn't much like that question, knowing they each had a history of using sex to cope. But he wanted, no needed, to feel alive too, to push aside the disappointment of the last two months and harshness of the last several hours.

Jett opened the door. "You lead the way home. I'll follow."

Delia brought the truck to a stop as Jett parked beside her. She drew in a breath, watching him circle to open her door. He held out his hand. "No talking starts now."

She followed him to the bedroom through the dark living room. With the door closed, he let go of her hand so he could turn on a lamp in the corner of the room. A small muscle twitched below the angular curve of his jaw as he walked back to her.

"Shhh," she said with a finger to her lips, watching his gaze sweep down to her mouth.

He nodded, then gently brushed her bangs aside.

She inhaled at the hot, hungry arousal on his face. Heat crept up her neck, his hand curving around, his thumb skimming the delicate skin beneath her ear.

He leaned in, his warm breath lingering just above her lips before he claimed her mouth in a sensual kiss. A rush of heat flooded her entire body and she braced herself, pressing her hands hard against his chest. His tongue brushed hers and he made a low noise in his throat. She sunk in when he deepened the kiss, clinging to his shoulders. Her body tingled with desire.

He broke their kiss, took both her hands, and pulled her as he slowly walked backward to the bed. Sitting, he drew her forward until she stood between his legs, his large hands spanning her hips.

Delia stared down at his handsome face before taking a step back. She pulled her shirt over her head. Reaching behind, she unclasped her bra and let it slowly slide down her arms. Her breasts were heavy and achy. Then she unbuttoned her jeans and pushed them along with her panties to the floor and stepped out.

Her heart skipped a beat when she stood naked before him. His look of awe made her feel delicate. Sexy. And oh, so feminine.

A small breathless whisper escaped her lips when his fingers glided around the back of her thighs, his hands holding firmly to her behind as he tugged her closer. He teased her tight nipples with his tongue. She arched, her fingers flexing as she held his shoulders again. His gaze drifted to hers as he cupped her breasts, then moved his hands to her hips, gently guiding her to take a step back.

Pulling off his boots, he then stood, his gaze holding hers, and swiftly removed his shirt and jeans and sat again. He crooked his finger, beckoning her forward, and skimmed his hand over her abdomen. Her muscles contracted, quivering at his touch. Her tiny gasp caused him to chuckle softly.

She was slick with heat. Her gaze fixed on his muscular thighs and the hardness of his arousal. A wide scar puckered skin near his left hip. Stepping forward, she ran a finger along a scar that ran from the base of his neck to the edge of his shoulder. She positioned her softness over him, opened her legs and lowered.

The only sounds were soft breaths and the slightest rustling of sheets at the rhythm of their rocking. With a slow and steady motion, she lifted and lowered, his hands gripping her hips, her arms around his neck.

Eye to eye, she shivered, her sex needy as he thrust, quickening the pace of their lovemaking. His kiss held a harsh desperation. Possessing. Demanding. Wanting.

She arched as waves of pleasure pulsed through her body, one after the other. Floating back down again, he cradled her head, kissing her lips, cheeks, eyelids and neck.

In a forceful move he swept her up in his arms and turned. She whimpered when he slipped from her body before laying her on the mattress. She hooked her legs around his hips and slid her fingers along his powerful back.

"Let me in," he said, breaking their silence, his voice sexy and impatient as he rose above her and re-entered. His rapid movements sped her along too, building with him toward the brink and she tightened her legs. With deep thrusts, he crushed his lips to hers, barely stifling his groan as he climaxed. She trembled through a hidden, more intense, orgasm pulsating her to completion a second time.

# Chapter 13

THE FAMILY GATHERED AT THE ranch two days after Annie died. Two days since he'd made love to his wife after months without. Two days that she'd been sleeping in his son's bed again. The story always the same.

"What if he wakes up scared?" Delia asked.

"Then one of us will go to him, but it can't be good to make the boy's sleep dependent on you being physically next to him all the time."

"I'm trying to be a good friend to him," she argued.

Whatever vulnerability she'd allowed the night Annie died was locked away again, and no amount of coaxing or kindness or arguing was getting through.

At the kitchen table, Jett held RJ on his lap with Delia, Ben, Jim and Sofia and Doc Cindy gathered. Leo and Kai and their children brought in chairs from the dining room and crowded around along with Rafe. The living room would have been more accommodating, but it always seemed the big Mannis family conversations happened at the kitchen table.

Annie hadn't wanted a funeral. She asked simply for the reading of a letter to RJ and the family that she'd written with Doc Cindy's help.

"There are three letters," Cindy said. "We're here to read the letter for RJ and the family. These," she put two envelopes on the table and slid them toward Jett and Delia, "are for each of you."

Jett picked up his letter and tucked it into his back pocket. "Thank you."

"I should read this later?" Delia asked.

"Whenever you're ready. It's just for you," Cindy answered and turned her attention toward RJ.

"RJ, your mom wrote a letter to you and I'm going to read it, okay?"

"Okay."

*"Dear RJ, I love you very much. Mommy is always so proud of you. The way you like to learn at school and play with your cousins."*

Cindy glanced at Kai with a tender smile.

*"I am proud of how kind you are to everyone you meet. How loving you are to me, your dad, and Delia. I want you to know that I'm okay now. You will be okay too because you have a family that loves you. Sometimes it may be hard because I'm not here. So, I'm leaving some directions for everyone."*

Cindy paused when Jett put a hand up for her to stop.

"RJ, do you understand what this note from your mom is about?"

He shook his head.

"She wants all of us to take care of you, and she's made a list about how we should best do that."

Cindy cleared her throat at Jett's nod to proceed.

*"Number one, I'd like Uncle Jim to teach you how to ride a horse someday and for your Aunt Sofia to take way too many photos of you riding."*

Jim took Sofia's hand. "We can't wait."

*"Number two, when your dad decides you're old enough, I'd like him to get you your very own puppy and build a doghouse together."*

RJ's eyes lit up. "I'm getting a dog."

Jett chuckled. "Sounds like it, buddy."

*"Number three, I hope RJ can keep spending as much time as possible with his cousins."*

"You bet," Leo answered quickly.

*"And…"* Cindy continued… *"get in on weekly pizza day with Aunt Kai, Uncle Leo, Will, Jocelyn, Aiden, Luke and Suze."*

Kai ruffled RJ's hair. "Always."

"Take it from me, you don't want to ever miss pizza day," Will added with a wink.

*"Number four, a boy needs to know how to fish and I'm hoping your Grandpa Ben will teach you."*

Ben nodded. "I wouldn't have it any other way."

*"Number five."* Cindy inhaled and put her hand on Delia's arm. *"Delia, you've already done for RJ what I hoped. You've given him your heart."*

"Oh my." Delia pressed a tissue to her eyes.

"Almost there." Cindy reassured the teary-eyed group.

*"RJ, Mommy wants you to play and be happy. To keep learning and to grow healthy and strong. And always keep your heart wide open to take in all the love around you."*

"Whew," Ben said as everyone wiped their tears. "How about you and I start right now, RJ. We could head out for a fishing lesson."

"Would you like to do that?" Jett tightened his arms around RJ in a hug before helping him off his lap.

"Come on." Ben held out his hand. "Let's see if the fish are biting."

Doc Cindy pushed her chair back. "I'm going to go now too and let you all have family time."

"Cindy," Jett said. "You are family. Thanks for everything you did for Annie. And for all of us today."

"You're welcome." She gave an easy wave and opened the back door.

"Papa Jack!" RJ ran to the door. "Are you coming fishing too?"

"Dad?" said Delia.

Jack Kincaid walked into the kitchen. "Hi, everybody," he said and squatted down to RJ's level.

"Come here and give me a hug, sport." He opened his arms. "I'd love to go fishing."

Ben came around the table his hand out to shake Jack's hand. "Glad you could make it."

"You'll all have to excuse me for a second first." Jack opened his arms again, taking Delia into a hug. "How are you holding up, kiddo?"

"It's been tough. I can't believe you're here,"

she said and stepped back.

"After all the phone calls I got inviting me, I feel like I know all of you." Jack put his hand out to each family member. "Jett, good to see you. I'm sorry it's under these circumstances. Jim, how are you? Rafe, it's been a while, you're looking good. And this must be Kai."

"Hi," Kai answered. "This is my husband, Leo, and my kids."

"What's your name?" Jack asked as he greeted each child before turning to Ben again. "I appreciate you inviting me to stay at the ranch. I hope I won't put you out too much."

"Not at all," Ben replied. "I'm looking forward to it. But I think we better get to fishing pretty quick before RJ leaves without us."

"Good idea," Jack agreed with a chuckle.

"How long can you stay, Dad?"

"I'll be here for a couple days. Maybe you and I can go to dinner later? If nobody minds me stealing Delia away?"

"Of course," Jett said. "We're glad you're here."

RJ, Ben, and Jack headed outside as Delia sat again. "So, who called my dad, besides Ben?"

Jim, Sofia, Jett, and Kai raised their hands.

"Thank you."

Later that night, when Delia was out with her father and RJ in bed, Jett sat in the guest room where Annie had stayed and read her letter to him.

*Dear Jett,*

*Who could know with our start that I would ever say these words – I love you as the father of our child.*

*Thank you for giving me the greatest gift of my life. When it feels like the right time, I had Doc Cindy help prepare the paperwork for you to change RJ's name from Reed to Mannis. All you need to do is sign too. Please know that I want this. Love and enjoy RJ enough for the both of us. – Annie*

The next morning, Delia and her father walked the property around Mercy Mountain Lodge.

"The aspens are incredible," Jack said. "With the mountains in the distance, this place calls to a person."

"That's what the family hopes for. That people will come here from all over and never want to leave." She chuckled. "Or at least that they'll make reservations every year to come back."

The path they were on ran on the southern side of the main lodge and led to four of the separate cottages in construction on the site.

"When will everything be completed?"

"Early next year. Jett says they want the buildings done prior to Thanksgiving, so that's just a couple weeks. It will take longer to paint and furnish them. They've already filled the main lodge with guests for Christmas. That was goal number one."

"I can't imagine that was hard," Jack said. "This place with snow will be breathtaking."

Delia stopped next to a tree with a sculpture of a mountain lion descending a rock.

"This is what I wanted to show you. Catherine Kendall Mannis' sculptures are installed all along the paths. In the spring, they'll be adding signs with photos of her sculpting or her sketches and notes so people can read about her work."

"That's marvelous. It doesn't surprise me one bit that this is all Sofia's idea."

"Me either." Delia took her dad's arm as they continued to walk.

"It's Jett's idea to name the cottages after the kids in the family, and Jim came up with naming the main room in the lodge after their mother. Catherine Hall. You know Jim, he just needed to get beyond the repairs for the lodge before he could be convinced about the creative side."

Jack chuckled. "That's why some of us are artists and some of us are…not. Have you missed your performing since you came out here?"

"No. I completely burned out, I guess." Delia shrugged. "I've missed you. Jim says you and he are meeting with some people in Four Bears tomorrow. What's that about?"

"The town is looking for someone to run for sheriff there next year."

Delia wrinkled her nose. "You? Small town sheriff?"

Jack tilted his head side-to-side. "I wouldn't be interested in the job if it was in Ashnee Valley."

"Really, why?"

"A bit too Mayberry. You don't need to repeat that out loud."

"I won't." Delia laughed.

"Four Bears has an edge to it. More crime too, unfortunately. Plus, it's on the verge of a comeback or so the folks there are playing it up to me.

I've been bored with early retirement."

Jack stopped walking and inhaled deeply. "I could get used to this blue sky."

"It's nice to see you excited. Won't it be hard for you to leave the house and New York?"

"I'm sure it would be." Her dad held gave her a pointed look. "It takes courage to cross a threshold. I haven't exactly demonstrated that to you or myself in a very long time. In a way you coming here inspired me."

"Me?" Delia put a hand to her chest.

Jack chuckled as they walked again. "Why so surprised? You've always been brave."

"Let's sit," Delia said when they reached a bench along the path. "Dad." She squeezed her eyes shut and puffed out a breath. "I threw myself into this new life and I'm so overwhelmed. Annie left a note for me and it's about adopting RJ. She wants me to let him call me Mama."

He put his arm around her. "Hey, now."

"What if I'm like her?"

"Who? Your mother? That's not possible. Your mom could never get out from under her addiction. I hoped for far too long and let you experience things I never should have."

"You did your best," Delia said. "She did too."

"No." He shook his head vehemently. "She didn't. You know, one of the things I've thought about on this trip is acceptance. Staying with Ben and listening to his struggle about coming to terms with Catherine's death has made me think too. It's taken him a lot of years, but now he has a new love with Patsy. He's happy." Jack sighed. "It's time for me to accept your mother for who she was and move on."

She wiped her eyes with the cuffs of her shirt. "So, Four Bears would be a second chance?"

"If I can get elected." Her father stood and put his arm out again for her to take. "I've never run for public office. That's what the meeting is about tomorrow. To see if I can win over some locals to support a campaign."

"I should come back with you to New York when you go." She shook her hair out. "Just to clear my head for a few days. Make one more trip before you sell the house. I'd be shocked if you don't charm your way to sheriff."

"You might think some more about whether that's a good idea right now," Her father suggested with a pat to her arm. "It won't be the last chance."

# Chapter 14

IF FORCED, JETT HAD TO admit that listening to Delia announce plans to visit New York this week didn't come as the shock it did to the rest of the family. He even smiled at the others around the kitchen table at the ranch, albeit with no pleasure.

"I tried to talk her out of this," Jack Kincaid told him that very afternoon before he left Ashnee Valley for the airport. And suddenly Jett and his father-in-law were in this thing together.

"I'm not going to fight her on it," Jett said to Jack then and again now to the group nervously glancing back and forth between Delia and him.

Ben rose from his chair. "I'm taking the kids outside." He exited through the swinging door to the living room.

"I'm staying at the table," Will announced and no one objected.

Jett glanced at each of them, wondering who would begin first. Kai collected plates and silverware as she spoke.

"RJ needs you both."

"It would only be for a couple days." Sofia came to her friend's defense, putting her hand on Delia's with a squeeze. "Right, Delia?"

It wasn't hard to recognize Sofia struggling by her half-hearted tone as she attempted to smooth the situation.

Delia stood, pushing her chair in toward the table. "I'm sorry for disappointing all of you."

Jett stared ahead when she left the room. Jim stopped Sofia, his hand gentle on her wrist when she got up to follow. "Hold on."

"But..."

"This family sticks together and that includes you."

"Jim, no..."

"I agree with Uncle Jim," Will interrupted, ignoring his father's admonishing shake of his head.

"Go on," Jett encouraged his nephew to speak.

"If she doesn't want to be here, then she should go. I'm sorry, Aunt Sofia. I know she's your best friend. But this is family, and we need to be here for RJ the same way we came together for Uncle Jim when he left the Army and the police force and Uncle Jett after his accident. We're lucky Uncle Jett is alive, and it seems to me he's been doing everything he can to stay sober and get back on his feet. He works hard. He's a good father. He puts RJ first."

Leo took hold of Kai's hand and an awkward silence settled over the group again.

"I admire him." Will sat back and stared down

at his lap. "I hope someday I can be half the father he is and that my dad is to me."

"Thanks, Will."

Jett glanced at Sofia. The loyalty she had for him warred against the loyalty to her friend, and it showed in every pained corner of her face.

"Go on, Sofia. Delia is family too and she needs you. I'll be fine."

It took everything Delia had to stay on course walking toward gate D2 for her flight to Minneapolis with a connecting flight to LaGuardia. Oh, to be so young and innocent like RJ last night when she'd explained her trip to him. Preoccupied with the promises of fishing the next day, he'd merely hugged her at bedtime. It was the first night that Jett slept in RJ's room, and she suffered a fitful night alone.

Determined, she'd put on her game face in the morning and for the ten thousandth time told herself this was for the best. The last thing RJ needed was to transfer his attachment from Annie to her and then her leave when her year was up.

She survived her own mother's death. Jett survived his mother's death. People survived their mother's deaths.

She stepped onto the moving sidewalk and pressed her hand to her queasy stomach. Over the paging system, she heard her name and a request to return to the security desk in the main terminal for a lost item. Glancing at her carry-on bag she wondered what could possibly be missing.

She made a U-turn and headed back the way she came, stopping once to rummage through her purse, pulling out her wallet, ticket, phone, sunglasses.

"I'm Delia Kincaid," she said stepping up to the young man smiling behind the security counter. "You paged me for a lost item?"

"Yes, indeed." She turned following his gesture and dropped her purse bringing both hands to her chest.

"Again? Dad, what are you still doing in Colorado? I thought you flew out yesterday."

"I'm here to talk some sense into you and I brought reinforcements."

Delia's jaw dropped open when Ben stepped forward.

*Ambushed.*

"I don't understand. My flight is about to board, and I was coming right to the house to see you. Ben…" Delia paused.

"Your dad is staying a few more days. I'm here to drive him back to the ranch and you home," Ben said.

"What?"

"I've rescheduled my flight. I've got a second meeting in Four Bears."

"That's great, Dad." Delia studied her father, looking for a chink in the armor, something to tell her this was all a crazy practical joke. "This almost seems like a mini-intervention."

The PA system crackled to life with another announcement.

"See there," Delia pointed a finger in the air,

"that's the call for my flight. I guess I'll now see you when you get back to New York."

She took a step back when both men closed in on her.

"Ben, would you give us a few minutes, please." Her father led her to a row of seats, gesturing for her to sit. "For a long time, it was you and me facing the world."

Delia crossed her arms. "That sounds like 'four-score and seven years ago.' I'll miss my flight."

"That's the point." He emphasized his answer with an impatient glare over the rim of his glasses. "I know about your agreement with Jett to stay for a year."

"You do?"

"He told me."

"Does Ben know too?"

"I don't think so and listen, whatever you decide ultimately, I'll support. No matter what. So when I ask you this next question, remember I said that. Are you sure you know what you're doing?"

This was the type of father he'd always been. Direct, and solidly in her corner. The same kind of father that Jett would be for RJ. The realization landed on her heart as both wonderfully freeing and catapulting her desperation to be right back in the thick of it all. In RJ's life. In Jett's arms.

Delia shut her eyes. "I've made a terrible mess of things. Jett is unlikely to want me back or near RJ after this."

"You may be right."

"Thanks, that's comforting."

"Honey, you're scared. Tell me what's really going on. I don't believe you're running from a kid like RJ. Is it Jett? Do you love him?"

"Yes." She puffed out a breath. "Suddenly, I'm on the verge of having the family I've always wanted."

"It's funny," her dad said as he pulled her in for a hug, "how getting what you want can be even more frightening than *not* getting what you want. You know, it's okay to change your mind and not get on that airplane."

"I'm glad you're here."

"Me too. What do you think? Ready to go back to Ashnee Valley? You can face the music and I'll ace my meeting in Four Bears, seeing as I want to live near my grandchild."

Her spiraling stomach lurched. It wasn't going to be as simple as stepping back into the picture after walking away.

"Hi, Nicki." Jett came through the back door and found RJ's babysitter at his kitchen table. "I thought Will was watching RJ this afternoon."

"He is. He's helping RJ change his clothes," she explained. "I just stopped by for a minute. My brother is coming to get me."

"All right then."

He dropped his tools by the door and took off his boots, entering the kitchen in socks that left soggy footprints on the dark wood floor. Filling a glass at the sink, he took his time quenching his thirst before turning toward the girl he knew his nephew pined for. When had she become womanly? He hadn't noticed until now. Fifteen going on twenty.

*God forbid, I ever have a daughter.*

"How's track going?"

"Fine. I'm starting cross-country skiing this winter. Jim's going to teach me to shoot a rifle. Maybe I'll try biathlon someday."

"That's impressive. You couldn't find a better coach than him, or Rafe. How's your brother doing? Staying out of trouble I hope."

"Mostly. He took his GED last week and passed. Eric is working for Sherriff Tanner."

Jett set his glass in the strainer. "You're kidding, doing what?"

She lifted her chin and pushed back her chair. "He's not perfect, but he's a good person."

Jett shook his head. "I shouldn't have made it sound otherwise. I'm the last person to talk."

"Daddy." RJ bounded into the room and wrapped his arms around Jett's legs.

Nicki glanced out the window and picked up her purse from the table.

"My brother is here." She knelt in front of RJ. "Bye, handsome."

RJ threw himself at Nicki, squeezing her in a hug. When she stood, she gave Will a little wave and sauntered past. "See ya."

The door slammed and Jett barely covered a "down boy" with his cough.

He poked RJ in the sides and ribs, tickling. "Now that RJ is five, he has a way with the ladies already, doesn't he?"

He picked RJ up and flipped him headfirst over his shoulder.

"Where should I put this sack of potatoes?"

Jett took off clomping through the house, bouncing RJ against his back through each room before tossing him in the middle of bed he once shared with Delia.

"Let's do it again." RJ jumped in the middle of the bed. "I want a piggy-back ride."

"I'll tell you what. You see if Will wants to stay for dinner, and we'll see about a piggy-back ride at bedtime, okay? Go on, I need to take a quick shower before we eat."

Later, after some 'wrastling' as RJ called it, plus reading a story about a brother and sister who traveled back in time to Egypt, he'd finally gotten his son to go to sleep.

Jett ran his hand over his lower back, massaging as he made his way to the living room. He took a seat on the other end of the couch from Will and tried to focus on the football game on TV.

"Wisconsin is winning," Will said.

"Hmm." Three more minutes clicked by on the game clock.

"So, you know Delia and her dad never left. They're back at Grandpa's ranch."

"I heard."

"That's kind of weird. Does RJ know?"

"Not yet."

Will hit the mute button as the game went into the half. "What are you going to do about her?"

Jett was positive he'd rather hear sports high

lights than have this conversation. Turnaround was fair play.

"Not sure. What are you going to do about your girl?"

"My girl?" Will laughed. "I don't have a girl and I don't plan on having one here. I have goals after I graduate. I don't need some hometown girl."

"Not even Nicki?"

"Especially Nicki. She's like a sister. I feel protective of her, that's all. She's had a rough family life."

"You don't look at her like a sister." Jett regretted voicing his observation as Will's expression shifted from uneasy to downright uncomfortable.

"She's one of many reasons I need to get the hell away from this town."

"In a big hurry it sounds. Jim mentioned you might enlist. Have you talked with your mom or dad about that idea?"

"Uncle Jim is a blabbermouth. I've talked to a couple recruiters for the Army," Will continued, "but I might be more suited for Navy. It's a way for me to pay for college. I want to go to medical school someday. Mom will freak."

Jett nodded. "That she will. But both your parents will be proud that you want to go into the same field as them."

The conversation dropped off for a minute. Will cleared his throat. "I think Delia needs to prove herself good enough for you and RJ."

"We're back to my life?" Jett chuckled. "That's how you would handle this, huh?"

"Yeah man or she'll own you."

Jett turned his gaze back to the TV. *She already does.*

# Chapter 15

Between the cold shoulder she got from every male Mannis and the pitying looks from the females, Delia was entirely out of her element at Suze's fifth birthday party.

Jett was polite but mostly avoided her. Even RJ monopolized her father at the dinner table. The group acted genuinely pleased with the possibility Jack Kincaid might run for sheriff of Four Bears.

*What a weird twist it would be if he stays, and I don't.*

She stole a glance at Jett only to find him staring right at her. His small smile did wonders.

The birthday girl crawled onto her lap and giggled. "I'm married to Uncle Jim."

"Hey, what about me?" Sofia asked and the crowd laughed loudly, causing Suze to startle.

Delia rubbed the little girl's back and tried to ignore the captive audience fixating on the scene. Maybe they were waiting to see if she would have a panic attack so they could chalk up another point on the giant mistake scorecard she imagined they were all keeping.

"Shhh." Suze stuck out her lower lip and put her adorable little hands to Delia's cheeks and leaned in for a kiss.

*Oh, that did it.*

She hung her head, breathing deeply, a warm tear running down her cheek. Kai lifted Suze gently off her lap and Ben pressed a tissue into her hand. Suddenly, everyone in her peripheral vision became busy collecting their coats and saying their goodbyes.

"Get your shoes on RJ. I need to get you home and to bed. There's school in the morning," Jett said.

As she stood, he pushed off the wall and headed straight toward her. His sexy walk made her physically ache for his touch. He stopped directly in front of her, not saying a word.

She held her breath, preparing for the worst. When he put his hand at the back of her neck and leaned his forehead to hers, she finally let the air out of her lungs.

"What am I going to do with you?" he whispered.

She averted her eyes and nodded, gripping his wrists as he held her cheeks with both hands.

"I'm not too happy with myself right now either," she said.

His hands slipped higher into her hair and tightened for a second before he stepped back.

"I want to come back home." She quickly wiped her cheeks at the sound of heavy footsteps in the hall.

"Watch it, that's my daughter you're making cry." Her father said as he entered the room.

"It's okay, Dad. I deserve it."

"Damn it, you don't." She flinched at the firmness of Jett's tone.

"You don't deserve this. Neither do I. I wish I was the man that could make you see that. Jack, can you keep an eye on RJ for a minute please?"

When her father left the room again, Jett held both her hands.

"Delia, I've spent the last fifteen years of my life living in the past or fucking-up the present and the future. I've made all the mistakes a man can. But you are breaking my heart. Who I am with you and RJ is the best of who I am. It's who I want to be. The two of you mean everything to me."

She frantically nodded.

"You're going to have to make up your mind and if you want me…show me."

Kai set up the tables at the Ashnee Valley Senior Center in assembly lines. At one end of each table were the cardboard boxes for packing holiday care packages to military on active duty. A variety of toiletries and non-perishable foods, as well as magazines, books, and phone calling cards, were neatly stacked.

Dragged along by Sofia to help get her out of her funk, Delia stood at the other end of a table. Her assigned task was to run the clear packing tape along the seam of each filled box before affixing the mailing label. Armed with her tape gun she waved the weapon at the appropriate moment during the instructions Kai gave to the group of volunteers.

The motley crew of all ages took their spots, lining the sides of each table and talking non-stop.

"How many of these boxes are we assembling, Kai?"

The woman who asked the question sat in a wheelchair and situated herself near Delia. She didn't wait for an answer before giving Delia direction.

"You can put the box on my lap after you put the tape on it." The woman pointed to Nicki. "This young lady will then hand me the labels. Won't you, Nicki?"

"You bet, Mrs. B."

Delia made eye contact with Sofia, who stood at a different table staffing the phone card and bison jerky station. A radio played holiday music as the group of mainly women chatted, and the assembly work began in earnest. Delia snacked on saltine crackers in between the moments when a filled box reached her. She secured each box with a satisfying stretch of tape and easily kept up. Mrs. B. was a fast worker as well, and the two women along with Nicki quickly fell into a comfortable rhythm.

Whenever one of the clusters of women burst out laughing at something one of them said, Delia smiled. Her mood lifted as rows of boxes were stacked along the back wall.

When Mrs. B.'s husband arrived to take her home, Nicki assumed tape duty, and Delia stood next to Sofia, putting items into boxes instead.

"What are you going to do?" Sofia asked her.

"I don't know. I'm not sure where I go in another few days when dad leaves."

"What did Jett say to you?"

The chattering died down and someone turned off the radio. The room fell silent. Several women stopped their movements entirely and stared her direction.

"What *did* Jett say to you?"

Delia recognized the woman asking from the sporting goods store downtown. She shifted uncomfortably at the crowd transfixed on hearing her answer.

"My, this really is a small town." She gave a friendly wink letting the group know she wasn't hurt by their harmless nosiness. "I'm not sure Jett would like all of you listening in."

"Of course, he wouldn't," another woman offered. "That's exactly why you should tell us."

Delia glanced at Sofia who shrugged.

Kai didn't miss a beat, her hands quickly loading another box with shampoo and soap before passing the box to her neighbor.

"Everyone here knows my little brother." She pointed at an elderly woman at table two. "That's Jett's kindergarten teacher."

She turned and pointed at a longhaired woman with a baby hanging in a sling across her middle. "That's his first kiss, Mary."

The woman tipped her head and went back to rubbing her hand on her baby's head.

Kai put her arm around the woman next to her and squeezed. "This is Sherriff Tanner's wife. She's brought Jett her hangover concoctions more times than she can remember. Right Gretchen?"

Gretchen bumped her shoulder to Kai's playfully. "Go on, we know who you're dealing with."

"Yeah, a man," the sporting goods woman said, and the group broke out in laughter.

Delia laughed with them. "Okay, well… he asked what he should do with me." She paused when several women made a tsk-ing noise in response.

"And then he said I needed to make up my mind."

The low murmur eventually broke forth into a series of exasperated exclamations and shocked expressions. Emboldened, Delia raised her eyebrows and added more.

"He wants me to show him."

That brought an even bigger response and Sofia gave her a warning look when she mimicked Jett as if he were a cross between John Wayne and King Kong.

*This is the best audience I've ever had.*

"That sounds totally like something my George would say too."

"Didn't you move all the way here from New York City to marry Jett?"

Sofia snorted. "He really said to show him?"

Delia nodded. "That he did."

"I'd go home right now," said a woman wearing a vest that looked like several potholders crocheted together, "and put on his hard hat and nothing else and wait for him at the dining room table."

"Like in that movie? Charlene, for God's sake, she's not a hooker!"

"Well, heavens, I know that."

Sofia set aside the box she worked on. "Let's take this discussion into the lounge and have our coffee break."

The group let out an excited whoop, and Delia marveled at the speed with which everyone filed out of the room. Several women pulled her along in the current and practically pushed her into a well-worn leather couch before surrounding her again.

"Thank you," Delia said when the potholder lady plopped the basket of saltines in her lap.

Kai stood at the front of the group. "I happen to know of a ranch house you should buy."

Sofia's whistle pierced the room. "Freeze. All cell phones down."

Several women giggled in response.

Delia lowered her chin. "Ben is selling?"

"You too, Charlene." Kai scolded as the potholder lady tucked her phone in her back pocket.

"Not exactly." Kai continued. "He's going to offer a trade with Jett. Dad moves into the cottage at the lodge. Jett takes the ranch."

"That's quite a trade. But what about you and Jim?"

"Jim's not interested in the ranch," Sofia said.

"Neither am I," Kai agreed. "It's always been

Jett who wanted it. The important thing is that it stays in the Mannis family. You're a Mannis. Besides, I'm only suggesting you buy the house, not all the property.

"Nobody move." Sofia left for a second, returning with a cardboard box. She circled the room collecting cell phones. "You'll get these back in an hour."

"If you're interested," Kai continued, "you should let him know right away. He's heading here with RJ and then driving up to Hawkeye to meet the guys for a weekend up north.

Delia stayed in the Senior Center lounge with Sofia while the rest of the women returned to the assembly line.

"This is pretty outrageous. I'd be shocked if Ben goes for it." Delia examined Sofia's slow growing grin. "That's creepy when you smile that way."

"You still have a lot to learn about Mannis men."

"Ben's in on this?"

"Of course. Kai already talked to him. Don't get a big head about it. It's not all for you and Jett. Ben's almost eighty. He can't take care of the ranch any longer. Besides, he's going to ask Patsy to marry him."

"Oh, that's so sweet. I wish my dad had someone in his life that way."

"Maybe Four Bears will be just the town for him. He's all alone in New York now. Even my parents moved away. I think he'd be the perfect person to be sheriff."

"So, I'll be a ranch wife and my dad will be the sheriff in the next town over."

"Only if you can convince your husband that he deserves you."

"It's the other way around."

"Don't be so sure. You might have had a little hiccup, but Jett's the one who needs to feel he's good enough for you too. This will put a little fight in his step."

# Chapter 16

"Huh." Jim held his phone in his left hand, reading the screen as he tried to open a can of soda with his other hand. He held his phone out so Rafe could read it.

"They're up to something."

"What?" Jett asked.

Rafe grabbed Jim's phone, read the text, and held it up to Jett. "They don't want us to get back early. That's what it says."

"I don't get it. Why?" Jett asked again.

"You weren't kidding when you said he wasn't the sharpest tool in the shed." Rafe handed the phone back to Jim.

"Shut up. What's Sofia's note mean?" Jett said.

"Where two or more women are gathered in your name, your ass is grass." Jim put his soda down. A fish tugged at the end of his line. "I got one, maybe we won't starve for dinner."

They were gathered in the tiny village of Hawkeye on the deepest part of the Talking Fish River outside of Ashnee Valley.

"I'm freezing," said Jett. "Do you think they're plotting something?"

Rafe shook his head. "Hell hath no fury like a scorned woman's gossipy town folk. You know where I'm going with this. What did you say to Delia anyway? Leo told me she was crying her eyes out the other night when he left your dad's house."

Jett's line tugged and he focused on trying to hook and reel in a fish before Jim got his out of the water.

"Nice, man." Rafe slapped Jim on the back. "That's a big one. What'd you get, Jett? Whoa, that's a keeper too. I better get in gear. The Mannis brothers are kicking my behind as usual."

"It helps if you put down your cigar and put a line in the water," Jett said pointing out the obvious as he took the hook out of the fish and placed it in the cooler. He put out both hands to receive Jim's fish and placed it in the cooler, closed the lid, and sat on top of it. After removing his gloves, he held his head in his hands. "Fuck."

"That bad?" Jim's voice held sympathy for once and Jett nodded.

They returned to the cabin an hour later. The wood stove burned, and a lively game of gin rummy was underway between Leo and his oldest son.

"I feel bad Grandpa isn't coming until later," Will said.

"He's bringing RJ. What were they up to when you guys headed here?" Jim asked.

Leo adjusted the unlit cigar in his mouth and sat

back, his chair creaking. "Heading to the Senior Center to eat pie with the women."

"What women?" Jett asked.

"All of 'em," Leo said.

Jett grimaced and put his coat and hat on again. "I'm going back out."

He slammed the door and raised his head to study the moon before stepping off the back step. Snow crunched beneath his boots as he made his way around the cabin, walking down the hill toward the shore again. Jamming his hands into his pockets, he turned when footsteps sounded behind him.

"Here, you forgot your gloves," Jim said when he caught up.

"Thanks." Jett pulled them on and rubbed his hands together. "I'm going down to the water, do you want to join me?"

"Sure." Jim turned on the flashlight on his phone to help light the way.

They walked along the edge of the river, stepping over rocks and downed tree branches before heading out on a short peninsula of flat rock.

"Dad's getting up there," Jim said.

"You know something I don't?"

His brother slapped him on the shoulder. "Not really. He just needs some more help getting around these days."

Jett faced the river. He'd always been comfortable letting Jim and Kai be the older ones, the ones responsible for most matters of family business. He had his own messed up situation with Delia and RJ.

*What am I going to do?*

"I've been talking with Sofia about setting Dad up at the lodge in one of the cottages." Jim continued. "It's not as good as taking him in our home."

Jett kicked the snow with the tip of his boot. "I could look after him if he was at the lodge if that's what you're thinking."

Jim shook his head. "Things with Dad and Patsy seem to be getting serious. I'm sure she'll be living with him soon. Besides, you're going to have to move out. We can't have the whole family living there. We need to rent as many cottages and rooms as possible to even have a chance at breaking even for the first few years."

"You know I can't afford to buy my own place yet. I guess maybe RJ and I can stay at Dad's house temporarily once he's moved to the lodge."

"That won't be possible, either. Dad just sold the house."

"He sold the ranch? When did that happen?"

"I'm not exactly sure what's going on. It was in the text from Sofia. I wanted to tell you before the others."

Jett stepped close to Jim. "Did your wife talk Dad into this crazy idea?"

"Watch whose wife you're talking about," Jim said with a shove. "Besides, why would she do that?"

"Cool it," Rafe suddenly stepped between them.

"Jesus, you're a stealthy bastard," Jett said. "I didn't even hear you approach."

"It was both your crazy wives, and everybody knows. It sounds like the whole town is involved. They convinced Ben to sell to Delia. Doc Cindy just narc'ed on them."

"What the hell?" Both men spoke the same sentiment.

"Wait, why would Doc Cindy tell you about it?" Jett asked.

Rafe wiggled his eyebrows. "We're forming a friendship. Maybe I should head back tonight."

"Right now?" They both asked.

Rafe grinned. "You boys are cute when you speak in unison."

"What the fuck is going on?" Jett mumbled and dropped his arms to his sides.

Jim grabbed hold of Jett to stop him as he marched after Rafe toward the cabin.

"There's no way Doc Cindy would throw the other women under the bus. Think about it. What *did* you say to Delia the other night? I'm guessing that got all the pots boiling."

Jett looked past his brother avoiding eye contact. "I told her if she wanted me, to prove it."

Jett shook off his brother's grip and kept up his quick pace to the cabin, warm air whooshing over him when he stepped back inside.

"Grandpa really sold the ranch?" Will said the second they closed the door. "That's been Mannis property for like a hundred years. How could he sell it like that, right out from under all of us?"

Jim sighed. "In case you forgot, Delia is a Mannis."

Leo slapped his hand on his knee and stood.

"We all know who the mastermind is, don't we?"

"Kai." The men groaned in unison.

"Mom?" Will said.

"Who does Grandpa check with before he makes any decisions?" Leo said. "There's no way he would do this unless Kai blessed it first. The question is what lit the spark?"

Jett frowned when all eyes turned his direction with glares of suspicion. He shoved clothes into his duffel bag, preparing to head back to Ashnee Valley.

"Why don't you share the ultimatum you gave Delia with all the boys here." Jim smirked.

"I told her to show me she's serious, okay?" His stupidity was met with a chorus of loud groans and a "hell yeah" from Will.

"I'm going back tonight. This is nuts."

Leo clapped his hands and rubbed them together like he was the evil scientist in a sci-fi thriller. "I say, no one goes anywhere. None of us. Even better, we call and say we're staying an extra day. Who's in?"

"I, for one, am never going back," Will said.

"Big talk, little man." Jim laughed but agreed with Leo's plan. "I'm cool with that idea. I'm better off fishing. Let the women hire movers to take Dad's furniture to the lodge. You should stay, little brother. You're pretty much guaranteed to make things worse by going back. Besides, Dad will be here with RJ in a while."

"We need more intel," Rafe said.

Leo rubbed his chin. "I think you're right."

"I know I'm right. Text your sister, Jim. The

cat's out of the bag already. She'll fill you in." Rafe moved to the recliner and pulled the lever propping his feet up.

Jim's phone buzzed immediately. "Incoming." He read out loud, "Tell Jett Dad only sold the house." Jim glanced up. "Kai put the word only in all caps and a bunch of winking emojis."

"That means the land and the animals are for sale. How much?" Jett asked.

"What's happening?" Will looked to each man.

Jim glanced up from his phone again. "One dollar."

"Sold," Jett answered. "There, see? I guess Delia will have to prove herself when I'm living on my land, which just so happens to be her new backyard."

Rafe chuckled. "I'd back track that attitude, Slick. You have some groveling to do."

"I know." Jett joined in laughing. "I'll head back first thing in the morning to surprise the new homeowner."

# Chapter 17

AMPED UP ON ASHNEE VALLEY woman power, Delia made the mistake of thinking the news of her buying Ben's house would cause Jett to come running back that very night. Instead, the men texted they planned on staying an extra day, and now she, Kai, and Sofia were left with the logistics of moving Ben out of his former home.

"You sure you don't want any of this?" Kai asked, walking around the house. "Dad doesn't want more than his favorite chair, TV, and bed. He's excited. Patsy is helping him pick out new furniture. They make the most adorable couple. I'm loving that the two of them will be the onsite people at the lodge." She laughed. "Imagine all the history of Ashnee Valley they can bore the guests with?"

Delia pulled another stack of books from a shelf and placed them into a box. She wanted to find something to keep so she didn't insult Kai or Ben.

"Um." She glanced around the living room.

Truth be told, she didn't want any of it. All the furniture came right out of the seventies and with how much sun the place got, most of the material on the couch and chairs, not to mention the curtains, was faded.

"You should keep the rocking chair in the guest room," Sofia said.

"Dad would love that. He made it for Mom when she was pregnant," Kai said. "He had a local artist do the carvings in it. She loved that chair. I mostly remember her sitting reading with Jett."

"Then you should have it Kai, not me."

"Jett will want you to rock all his babies in that chair."

Delia loaded more books off the shelf at twice her original speed. "*All* his babies." She rolled her eyes.

Sofia snickered. "How many Kai? I'm guessing all boys."

Delia ran her hand over her belly. "Don't answer that."

"Oh my God." Sofia covered her mouth with both hands. "You're pregnant."

Kai tilted her head. "I've been kind of wondering. You were eating an awful lot of saltines yesterday. Are you?"

"Let's go to the pharmacy and get a pregnancy test to be sure," Sofia said.

Delia slouched down on the couch. "That won't be necessary."

"This is so exciting." Sofia clapped. "How far along are you?"

"Eight weeks. You can't say anything." Delia

quickly lifted her gaze to each of them. "Jett doesn't know." She dropped her shoulders. "He's so fed up with me."

"He's far from fed up with you," Kai said. "But you did just attempt to leave."

*Ouch.*

"Do you think he's picking a fight with Delia, using the whole prove-it-to-me thing on purpose to test her?" Sofia said.

"No. But maybe he doesn't trust all this," Kai said. "I mean, that's partly because he's a guy and his pride is hurt. Everything came at him so fast in the last year. If he's not sure he can keep up with you, Delia, he'll never be sure you'll stay."

She struggled to maintain eye contact. "It's okay," she assured her friend with a pat to her knee when Sofia sat down on the couch next to her. To Kai, she said, "Keep going."

"He knows what you bring to him. You're smart. You're beautiful. You're loving with his son. You even nursed his ex-lover before she died. What does he offer you that no other man can? It's possible he's slowing everything down, so it doesn't hurt so much if you leave for good."

Sofia pressed her lips together. "I've never had drama like this with Jim."

"Oh, shut up." Delia chuckled.

Kai rolled her eyes. "Please."

"He really doesn't think he's good enough? He survived a near fatal car accident. He's done physical therapy for over a year to fully recover. He's sober. He's leading the construction at the lodge. He's raising a son, who is adorable. What do I do?"

Kai packed items again. "Let him show you. Make it safe for him. Sofia, help me out here."

"You could wear sexy stuff around the house and ask him to fix the drain or something."

Delia squinted. "That sounds outdated and completely stupid. I'm not going to bring him his slippers in a French maid outfit, so he feels better about his manliness."

"Of course, you're not. He'd be on to you in two seconds anyway." Kai snickered. "He'd really dig the outfit though. Okay, that is weird I said that about my little brother. I'm not sure we can tell you what's best to do."

Delia paced in front of the couch, then stopped and crossed her arms. "Why are you making that face at me, Sofia?"

Sofia gritted her teeth. "I am neither outdated nor stupid."

"Oh, really now?" Delia tilted her head. "Wear sexy clothes and ask him to fix the drain? Besides, I never said *you* were those things."

"Obviously," Sofia said with a rapid series of blinks, "it is a flower that attracts the bee."

Kai shrugged.

"I don't get it. You're saying I'm the flower? Jett calls me the honeybee." Delia tapped a finger to her own chest. "I am the honeybee!"

"Actually, it's just plain honeybee." Jett's deep voice filled the air as he stepped into the room. "Not *the* honeybee, that sounds a bit pretentious." He took off his hat. "Is everything okay here?"

Kai squeezed her brother's arm. "It will be."

"You're up, Honeybee." Sofia followed Kai out of the room.

"Everything is fine," Delia rubbed the back of her hand across her forehead.

"I didn't mean to interrupt."

She smiled. "You didn't."

"Good." He nodded.

She returned his nod. "Good."

"I'm putting my trailer on the property." He headed back to the door and turned around. "You may own this house, but I bought the land and the animals, so I need to be here to take care of the ranch."

*Could it be this simple? He takes care of the ranch and I...* She realized he was still talking to her.

"If you need anything, I'll take care of it. If anything comes up."

"Thank you."

"Anything," he repeated.

She lifted her chin to avoid smiling like a complete fool. "All right."

His eyes swept over her, examining every inch before continuing. "I don't know if I have a right to, but I want something from you."

*Good lord. If you ask me to run off the edge of a cliff I will.*

She clasped her shaky hands behind her back. "What is it?"

"Let me court the hell out of you."

She lifted her eyebrows. "Let you?"

He nodded. "I love you, Honeybee. Let me prove to you how much."

A small breathless whisper escaped her lips and

she smiled. "That's *The* Honeybee to you."

He stalked across the room to stand in front of her, leaving less than an inch between them.

"*My* Honeybee."

"Oh." His words sent an electrifying flush of warmth to her core. "Um, okay."

*Can I not utter a single coherent sentence?*

He swept his thumb across her bottom lip. "Not like that. We're equal in this. We'll keep working at this marriage until we're both on top of it together. At least both on top in the daylight." She enjoyed his flirtatious leer as he leaned in to buss her cheek with a kiss.

"Where's RJ?" she called after him as he walked to the door again.

"Jim's dropping him off here tomorrow morning. RJ thinks we're going to play ranch hands or something. He's excited. We'll be fine in the trailer."

"Jett." She wrung her hands. "This feels strange. You should be in this house. I got talked into this crazy idea and it was a mistake. This is wrong. You stay and I'll go. I'll stay in the trailer."

"No, ma'am." He pulled his chin back with a laugh. "Are you kidding me?"

"What do you mean? I could do it." She straightened her back. He crooked his finger beckoning her across the room.

"What?" she said when they stood toe-to-toe.

"Have faith in this, that's all we need to do right now."

"It's awkward."

He chuckled. "I suppose it's a little on the

unusual side. But it could be fun. We never did date."

"That's what you want?" She searched his eyes. "You want us to date?"

"There's nothing that says we can't hit the rewind."

She considered his words carefully. "So, when's our first date?"

"Well, I haven't asked you yet."

She gave him a sassy look. "What if I ask you?"

"I'm game. Give it a shot, Honeybee."

"Would you…"

"Yes," he interrupted with a slow-growing grin.

"Don't you want to know what we're going to do?"

He opened the door and stepped outside. "Doesn't matter." He shrugged. "The answer is always going to be yes."

"Okay, then I'll see you and RJ at six for supper on Sunday."

"You're making me wait another whole day?" he asked.

She leaned on the doorframe and tilted her head side-to-side. "I'm hard to get."

Sunday morning, Delia quickly shut off the washing machine and jumped back just in time to avoid her feet being swallowed by the soapy water flooding the floor. The series of shakes and bangs had jolted the washer about three inches from the wall. It didn't take a genius to tell in hindsight that cramming all the kitchen curtains and tablecloth into the small machine at once was a bad idea.

Taking off her shoes, she stepped tentatively into the water and bent over the top of the machine to see if a hose had come loose. She unplugged the electrical cord, cursing how stupid that probably was while standing in water. At the call of her name from upstairs, she tip-toed through the water, grabbing and tossing an old towel on the floor to soak up some of the overflow.

"Coming," she shouted as she headed up the stairs. "Jim. Oh, thank God."

"I just dropped RJ off with Jett," he said with a glance out the kitchen window.

"Good. I'll go see him in a few minutes. First, can you help me? The washer is flooding the basement."

"Let's see what we got," he said, crossing through the kitchen.

She followed him down the stairs, rattling off all the items she'd crammed into to the washer, then proceeded to re-enact the banging and crashing sounds that brought her to the basement. She concluded by nodding toward the pool of water.

He leaned over the top of the machine.

"I unplugged it."

Jim nodded.

"Do you see the problem?"

Jim grunted.

"I shouldn't have put all those items in at the same time. I was trying to get the curtains washed and hung up and the tablecloth ready for dinner tonight. It must have gotten off balance. Poor thing was shaking all over and practically tried to walk itself across the room."

"Uh huh."

"Do you think that's what caused it? Is it something you can fix?"

"Right now?" Jim grabbed more old towels and threw them down on the floor to soak up the water. "No."

"But…"

"You know who's good at fixing stuff? The guy out in the trailer in your yard."

"I'm sure he is." She followed Jim up the stairs. She leaned on the counter, wiping her feet with a paper towel. She glanced at him, her smile falling at his glare.

"He's your husband."

"I'm aware of that."

"Are you?"

They scowled at each other in mutual annoyance. She crushed the paper towel and chucked it into the waste can across the room.

"Would you excuse me now? I have to start preparing, seeing as I have a *date* with my *husband* tonight."

"Crap. I didn't know that." Pulling off his hat, he scratched his head. "I'm not good at doing this."

She put her hands on her hips. "I'm not sure what you are doing, but you suck, actually."

He slid the rim of his hat back and forth in his hands. "He's my little brother. I love him. I'm worried about all this."

"Jim…"

He rubbed the back of his neck. "No matter what you do, he's going to fight for you. He loves you. And I know I don't know everything about your life before now, but I think you deserve that kind of love as much as he deserves to have you and RJ to give his love to. I sure as hell know RJ deserves you both. All this entire family wants to do is take you in. We want to be family to you, sis. To you and your dad."

Delia lost it with big slobbery sobs and hiccupped laughter. "Wow, I take back that whole thing about you sucking."

When she approached, he took a step back, holding out his handkerchief. "Don't cry."

"You called me sis."

"Did I?"

She wiggled her eyebrows. "That means you love me too."

"Whoa…I guess. Like a sister. Like that."

His wary expression only made her enjoy pushing further. "I've never had any siblings. Sofia's the closest thing I have to a sister."

"Well, there you go." Jim put his hat back on his head. "One big happy family."

"Jim." She blocked his way to the back door. "I'm just a girl, standing in front of a boy, asking him to be her brother-in-law."

"Oh, for fuck's sake. Even I know that's from a movie."

She flung her arms wide and hugged him. Stepping away, she blew her nose then stuffed the handkerchief back in his shirt pocket.

He chuckled as he opened the door to leave. "That's disgusting."

## Chapter 18

"STAND STILL, RJ." JETT SMILED in the bathroom mirror as he stood behind his son. He'd put RJ up on the closed toilet seat so he could help him tie his first tie. "Cross the right over the left. Good. Wrap it around now." He pointed at the loop where RJ should pull the tie through.

"I got it. I'm wearing a tie, Daddy, just like you."

"Women can't resist a sharp dressed man, remember that." Jett lifted RJ and set him outside the bathroom. "Don't mess up your clothes, we're leaving in about five minutes. Just give me another second."

He went to the back of the trailer and closed the door. Opening the drawer to the bedside table, he took out two condoms, then put them both back. *Damn.* This was not going to be the sort of date that ended in getting naked with Delia no matter how much he wanted that. For one thing, RJ was going on this date, and second, he was supposed to be courting the woman, not trying to get in her panties immediately.

Emerging from the bedroom he stopped at the window as his brother and Nicki drove up. Great, all he needed were more witnesses to his courtship of his wife. Jett stepped outside.

"Hi," he greeted them as they emerged from his brother's truck. "Hey, sweet pea," he said as Jim helped Suze out of the backseat, and she ran toward him.

"What are you all doing here?"

"Well, shit," Jim said.

Suze pointed. "Potty mouth."

"Don't worry, I'm not staying. Sofia thought Nicki could take over at some point and babysit RJ and Suze, so you and Delia could have some quiet time. I thought you knew the plan."

"Nope, but it's a good plan."

"I'm going to dinner!" RJ announced. "I don't need a babysitter. Suze is a big baby, but I'm not."

"Russell James." Jett issued a warning look. "You will only go to dinner once you apologize to Suze. Neither of you are babies."

The corners of RJ's mouth drooped. "I'm sorry, Suze."

Unfazed, Suze said, "I'm hungry."

Nicki stepped forward. "I thought you and I could play until RJ comes back from dinner. We can have a snack."

"I'm hungry," Suze repeated.

Jim pulled off his hat and scratched his head at this new development. Jett got out his phone from his pocket and texted Delia.

**Jett:** Okay if Suze joins dinner? I can explain

later.

**Delia:** Of course.

"You can both go." Jett turned to Nicki. "Are you okay hanging out here for an hour before these rug rats come back? You can eat or drink anything in the fridge. When they get back you could watch a movie. The TV is small, but it works."

"Sure," Nicki answered, lowering herself on the couch already absorbed in her phone.

When the gang minus Nicki stood outside the trailer, Jim asked what time to pick up the girls.

"Nine o'clock," Jett answered.

"Have fun on your date, bro."

Holding both kids' hands he walked the driveway toward his father's house. How ironic that the house he grew up in now belonged to his wife. Reaching the steps to the backdoor, nerves got the better of him, and he let go to wipe his hands on his pants before knocking.

His affection for this woman slammed into him as she wiped her hands on a dishtowel and propped the door open. He followed the kids inside, willing his feet to move forward when all he wanted to do was press her body against the wall so he could take everything he wanted.

"Hi," she said.

"Hi," he answered, feeling increasingly like a pimply teenager. Straightening his shoulders, he shook off his nerves and examined the woman in front of him. She took his breath away in a pale pink dress.

"You look so beautiful."

She leaned into him and squeezed his bicep. "Good thing we have chaperones tonight because you look good enough to eat, cowboy," she whispered.

"Delia…" His voice came out more a growl, and he chased it with a mumbled "fuck" when he took in the telling flush of desire on her cheeks.

"What's for dinner?" RJ asked.

Delia laughed softly and went back to the kitchen to stir a huge steaming pot on the stove. When she gestured for Jett to take his place, he joined the kids at the table.

"We're having spaghetti and salad." She donned potholder gloves and carried the pot to the sink to pour the contents into a strainer. As the noodles steamed in the sink, she knelt next to Suze's chair.

"And I'm so glad you're here too, young lady. I made a ton, and we need all mouths on deck." She kissed the top of Suze's head and ruffled RJ's hair, but barely made eye contact with him.

*That won't do.*

He crossed the room to stand next to her. "Can I help?"

She put the pasta in a casserole dish then poured sauce over it. "You could put the spaghetti in the oven. I need to finish making the salad."

He switched sides with her to reach the stove. As he passed, he gently squeezed her hip and let the touch of his hand linger on the small of her back. He picked up the casserole dish, glanced her way, and caught her looking right back.

"What?" she asked.

He set the dish down again. "I'm getting lost in the moment. This," he said with a gesture toward the table. "The kids, the meal, everything smells great. You look amazing. Patience isn't really my strong suit. I'm trying to keep my hands to myself."

"Me too," Delia pressed her lips together.

"Yeah? You feel it too?"

She went back to her salad making, but he could see the way she tried not to laugh.

"You want to feel it?" His cock grew against his zipper.

"Stop." She giggled. "Put the spaghetti in the oven, Jett."

He did as he was told and returned to the table, just in time to catch Suze's glass of milk before it tipped over. Taking a deep breath, he tried focusing on the children, who he'd briefly forgotten were in the room. RJ and Suze both sported black olives from the relish tray on the ends of their fingers.

During the meal he sighed when Suze eventually accomplished spilling her milk all over her plate. Delia patiently cleared the mess and set a new plate as if none of it bothered her in the least.

*I love this. Every damn bit. I want to be at this table each night, sitting across from this woman.*

He forked the last of his food impatiently, frustrated that his simple desires might not be enough.

"I want this." His words blurted out more forcefully than he intended but he barreled on anyway. "I want this life. Maybe you'll go back to your career, Delia, and maybe you'll have to be gone for months at a time. But we can make it work. We'll make it work. I want you and this family and this future."

He banged his hand on the table causing RJ to jump and Suze to cry.

"Oh, shoot."

He immediately leaned to pick Suze up, setting her on his lap. "Hey, sweet pea. I didn't mean to frighten you." He rocked his niece. "Let's send the kids to see Nicki. I'll help you clean up. After that I want to kiss you."

RJ wiggled making smoochy noises and Suze giggled.

"You think that's funny?" Jett tickled under Suze's chin. "RJ, can you and Suze go down to the trailer together? You take Suze's hand and don't let go. It's after eight o'clock so you can watch one TV show with Nicki and then it will be bedtime."

RJ and Suze scrambled to put their jackets on.

"Straight to the trailer," he said as a last reminder. "No letting go of each other's hands."

The backdoor slammed as the kids took off. He moved with purpose, joining Delia as she stacked dishes and collected napkins and utensils from the table.

"Should you watch them go around the corner?" she asked.

"Nah, they're only out of sight for a second. Besides, I'm on a mission. This is going to be the fastest kitchen clean up ever."

She picked up her pace when he did, and they

were soon laughing in competition. Delia ran from the table to the counter, then poured soap in the sink and filled it with hot water.

Jett put his hands on her hips and turned her around. "I don't ever want to date you again," he said and slammed his lips to hers.

When Jett had cradled Suze, resting his forehead on hers, that's when Delia surrendered completely. She couldn't wait to tell him about her pregnancy. There would be no going back once he knew. Time to cross a threshold with courage, as her father put it.

Jett kissed her with so much pent-up frustration and lust, her knees buckled. His arms circled, holding her tight against him.

Coming up for air she made her own admission. "I want this too. I want this life and I want you."

"Forget dating."

"Right." She nodded enthusiastically as he picked her up, her legs circling his waist, and carried her out of the kitchen and down the hall to the bedroom. He set her on her feet again.

"I love you, Delia. You have every part of me, my body, my heart, my soul. I've never wanted my life more than I do right now. My life with you and RJ. I'll do whatever it takes to make you happy."

"I love you too."

Jett's phone ringing brought a smirk to her lips. "You should check if it's Nicki."

He turned it so she could see the caller. "It is."

He had one hand on the phone and other to her cheek, caressing with his thumb.

"Hey, what's up Nicki?" He leaned forward and kissed her nose and below her ear before his head snapped up. "What do you mean, where are the kids?"

Delia's heartbeat picked up pace. She glanced at the bedside clock.

"We sent them down there about ten minutes ago. They didn't show up?"

She could hear every word on the other end of the line as Nicki confirmed the worst.

"No. I was only calling because I didn't know if you'd even need me to babysit tonight. I know they wanted to watch a movie before bed."

Delia motioned for Jett to hand her the phone. Pressing the mute button she said, "You go. I'll talk to her and follow." She put the phone to her ear as Jett left the room.

"Nicki, it's Delia. He's on his way. Don't worry, I'm sure they just got distracted, and we'll find them right outside the door. I'm on the way too, okay?"

She raced around the house looking for her shoes and finally found them, then slammed out the door. Running across the driveway, she headed toward the small barn the trailer was parked behind. Darkness had fallen completely. It would only get harder to find the kids as each minute ticked by.

She looked left and right as she walked straight to Nicki, who was outside the trailer calling the kids' names. Where had Jett gone?

"I'm so sorry," Nicki said.

"It's not your fault. Where's Jett?"

"He went to the stable. He wants me to stay put in case the kids return while you and he head out on horseback."

"But…"

# Chapter 19

"I CAN'T RIDE A HORSE, JETT."

"Now isn't the time to be worried about your technique, Delia. Time is ticking and we need to get to the pond. RJ's fishing rod is gone from where it was leaning on the trailer earlier."

"Oh God, Suze. Does she even know how to swim?"

"No." He was all business and she ached at having to tell him about her pregnancy this way. He tried to hand her the reigns.

"Jett, I can't. I'll have to stay at the trailer, and you take Nicki. I can't. I… the doctor said."

"What idiot doctor told you that?" He tightened the saddle strap and walked the horse to Nicki instead. "What kind of doctor would tell you not to ride a horse? This is a family emergency, Delia."

His words were curt, and she couldn't let him go on thinking she didn't care enough about RJ and Suze to do whatever was necessary.

"An obstetrician," Delia said and waited as her

words sunk in.

A huge grin broke across his face as he marched to her and pulled her into his embrace. "I love you so much. You and I are having a serious talk when I return." He gave her a quick kiss and then said, "Nicki, get on the horse and let's go."

He mounted his horse and stared down at her. "Everything is going to be okay. Do you understand?"

She nodded. The two horses raced toward the pond as she stood on the steps to the trailer.

Once she could no longer hear hoofbeats, she absorbed silence. Slowly, the rustling of leaves in the trees re-engaged her ears. She sat on the step, wrapping her arms around herself at the chilly evening.

When Jim pulled into the driveway, she walked with purpose toward his truck.

*How can I tell him we were so careless?*

It struck her that Kai had no idea her little girl was in any danger. Delia would not survive if something happened to Suze or RJ or her babies. She instinctively put her hand to her belly.

"I didn't expect to have you greet me," Jim said. "How was dinner?"

"The kids are missing," she said opening a floodgate of words. "RJ and Suze are missing, and Jett and Nicki took off on horseback to the pond because RJ's fishing pole is gone, and he's been wanting to show everyone his fishing skills and now he probably took Suze and it's dark and she doesn't know how to swim and I'm pregnant. Jim, I'm not fit to be a mother or have any responsibilities." She sucked in a shaky breath.

"Whoa, slow down. How long have the kids been missing?"

"I don't know, maybe twenty minutes."

Jim put his hands on her shoulders looking past her as she stared up at him. *He won't even look at me.*

"They're okay."

"No." She shook her head. "It's dark and they're too little to be down by the water alone and I don't have any right thinking I could be a mother. I'll never forgive myself and…"

Hands on her shoulders, Jim turned her as two horses headed back with four riders.

"They're fine."

She grabbed one of Jim's hands and placed several kisses on the back of it.

"Delia, you need to stop that right now or that husband of yours is going to punch me in the nose when he catches you slobbering on me."

"Oh, thank God." Delia took off running.

In the next minutes, two more trucks and a jeep pulled up in the driveway.

"I may have texted everyone," Nicki said as she dismounted.

The entire family talked at the same time, hugging, and kissing on RJ and Suze. The chattering only came to a halt when Sofia restored sanity with one of her loud whistles.

"Thank you," Jett said to her. "Okay everybody, it's time to call it a night. You can go home."

Jim laughed. "We're not leaving. We understand you have some big news, and we're not going until we get the whole story."

"I don't think it would be fair to make it a group announcement," Delia said looking at each person.

"I may have spilled the beans a little," Nicki admitted.

Will cleared his throat and held up his phone to read Nicki's text. "O. M. G. RJ and Suze went for a fishing trip on their own and are so totally busted. Plus, Delia is prego."

When Delia crumpled, covering her eyes, Jett caught her up in his arms. "It's okay."

"Delia," Ben said.

"Dad, what are you doing here?" Jett asked.

Ben stepped forward from the group. "I'm standing in my former driveway in the dark and it's way after my bedtime."

Delia studied Ben's amused expression. Behind him Kai swayed, rocking her daughter Suze in her arms. Will and Nicki had their heads together studying something on a phone, no longer paying attention to the adults. RJ held his Uncle Jim's hand and Sofia nodded.

"Tell us the news," Ben encouraged.

Jett squeezed his hands on her shoulders then spread them possessively across her belly, his rich laugh enveloping her. Soon everybody laughed and the tension from the night lifted and floated up.

So, she told the family. *My family.* About bringing another baby into the fold next spring.

Delia turned to Jett. "You'll need to build another cottage so we can name it after them."

She winked at Sofia whose mouth dropped open in a gape at her slip of the tongue.

It was in her rights to save an extra surprise for Jett first and when they were alone again.

Inside, after everyone left, Jett drew a bath for Delia, and set a glass of chocolate milk on the edge of the tub. She had a baby to feed after all.

He tucked RJ in bed, with a kiss and a promise of extra chores come morning along with a lecture about responsibility and the proper way to look after his cousin Suze.

He stopped at the bathroom when Delia called his name and stuck his head in the room.

"Hey, do you need something? You didn't drink your chocolate milk yet."

"I'll share it with you. I was hoping you'd join me."

"Oh yeah?"

She waved her hand beckoning him into the room. "Yes."

He whipped off his shirt and unbuckled his belt.

Delia wiggled her eyebrows. "Slow it down, cowboy. Let a girl take it all in."

"Very funny." He pushed his jeans and underwear down, stomping and kicking his pants from his ankles in an exaggerated way. He settled into the tub, facing her, his legs extending in the tub on the outside of hers.

"Are you okay?" he asked.

"I panicked earlier when Jim showed up and

before you were back with the kids. I was sure I wasn't fit to be a mother. I'm still not entirely confident, but another part of me can't wait to meet our baby soon."

"How soon?" He asked.

"In May."

"When were you planning to tell me?"

She scooted across the tub, her thighs sliding over his, her legs bent so she could straddle him.

"When?" He urged putting his hands on her waist.

"Tonight. I wanted it to be our news, just you and me. Not your entire family."

He moved his hands to cup her breasts and she breathed in sharply. "Don't touch my nipples. They're so sensitive these days."

He bent his head and kissed each breast everywhere else, stilling her hips when she rocked against his erection. He wasn't making love to her in a tub tonight.

"I have to be honest," he said. "I wish I was the only one who knew about the baby too." He shrugged. "I don't know why, other than I want to be the one to idolize you first."

She chuckled. "I do like attention."

He lifted her up and off his lap. Standing, he grabbed a towel to hand to Delia and another that he used to rub down his arms and across his chest.

"Tonight, it can be just you and me and the babies," she said.

"You, me, and the babies." He stepped out of the tub. "Sounds perfect, although I happen to know RJ would not enjoy being referred to as one of the babies." He fastened the towel around his waist.

"I'm not talking about RJ." Delia stepped out of the tub. "You see, there's a little more to the story. A part I haven't shared. Not yet." She patted her belly. "I guess there are two babies in here. That's why the doctor says I have to be extra careful."

When she went to wrap the towel around herself, he stopped her and knelt on the bath rug bringing his hands to her hips.

"That. Is. So. Damn. Sexy." He emphasized with a kiss to her stomach after each word. "Is this wrong?" He glanced up. "That you carrying our babies makes me want to worship your body all night long?"

"You won't find me complaining." She pulled his hair with a playful tug before sauntering out of the bathroom.

He considered following on his knees but didn't want to waste any more time. He entered the bedroom, threw off his towel, and belly flopped on the bed next to her, cracking up when she yelped.

"Have your way with me."

She bit her lip, her cheeks reddening.

He lifted on his elbows. "I love that I make you do that."

"What?"

"Get all hot and bothered."

"Shush," she said. "Turn over."

"Yes, ma'am," he said enthusiastically and

flipped from his stomach. He scooted up the bed resting against the headboard, his hands behind his head.

"Quiet," Delia whispered.

"We're good at quiet, aren't we, Honeybee?" He slid down on the bed, holding her hips when she straddled him, hovering.

"I love you. Husband."

"I love you too. Wife."

Delia put a finger to his lips as she lowered. "No talking starts now."

# Epilogue

*Five years later…*

"Jett," Delia whispered, waving her hand for him to join her at the entry to the living room. "Come here, you need to see the girls."

"What is it? I have to get back outside to RJ. We're almost done with the second doghouse."

"Shhh!"

He stuck his head around his wife's and peeked at their twin daughters swaying and singing along with music on the TV. They were the spitting image of Delia with their blond hair and sun-kissed skin.

"Now you've let it all go to your head. They've heard you sing that song their whole life. Of course they can sing it."

"Not that," she whispered. "Listen carefully."

"Are they doing what I think they're doing?"

Delia nodded like a crazy person. "Jett, they're harmonizing." She jumped up and down silently clapping her hands together.

"Holy shit."

"Holy shit is right," She repeated and skipped around the kitchen. "Isn't this a hoot? Even RJ can carry a tune and he's getting so good on the guitar."

Jett chuckled at her enthusiasm. "You know they're five, right?" He tried to wrap his arms around her, her swollen belly an obstacle. "Lord, woman, you are about to pop."

"I know. This is it, Jett. No more singers for the band."

"That's what you say now, but somehow you keep jumping me and impregnating yourself." He wiggled his eyebrows.

She ignored him, her enthusiasm bubbling back up. "Maybe I can write some songs for the girls and see how far they can take this harmonizing thing."

The backdoor slammed and nine-year-old RJ huffed his way inside.

"Dad, I've been waiting for like *two hours* for you to come back outside so we can finish the dang doghouse and go pick up the dang puppy."

"I think it has been more like five minutes, tops," Jett said. "But I gotcha, buddy. I'm coming."

He kissed Delia and held the screen door for his son.

"We're outnumbered pal, sometimes the girls need attention. Your Mama and I were watching your sisters singing."

"Whoop-dee do," RJ said with all the interest of an older brother who had better ways to spend his time.

"Oh!" Delia bent forward, her hand held beneath her belly as a splash of water hit the kitchen floor.

Jett let go of the door and caught her beneath her elbow, his arm coming quickly around her back.

"Steady," he said. "That's good. Let's walk you over to the counter." He leaned away when she gave him a no-nonsense glare.

"If you talk to me as if I'm a horse you're training like you did when the girls were born, I will kick you in the you-know-what, Jett Mannis."

"I love you, Delia." He glanced at the floor again. "From the looks of things, we better head to the hospital now.

"Olivia and Evelyn," he called into the other room, "turn off the TV and get ready, your mama is having the baby today. RJ, grab the bag in our bedroom next to the closet door."

Delia straightened, still letting Jett hold her arm as she pushed dishtowels off the counter and plopped them over the wet spot on the floor.

"When will you start calling the girls Livy and Evie, like everyone else does?"

"Never." Jett chuckled. "Okay, are you ready for this, Honeybee?"

"As I ever am," Delia answered. "Whose phone is ringing?"

Jett smiled at his nephew's name on his cell phone. "It's Will. Hey, Dude. Are you back in town? We're on the way to the hospital. We're having the baby. Looks like you've arrived in Ashnee Valley just in time. Call your mom and have her tell everyone else. Who knows, maybe they'll even let you be in the delivery room, seeing as you're a medical student." Jett's laugh boomed at something Will said. "Okay, yep, we'll see you there."

He held the door for the girls shuffling by with their little bags packed with stuffed animals and books. RJ stomped out the door.

*No picking up their newest rescue dog. Poor kid.*

"RJ," Delia called after him, "will you please help the girls buckle into their booster seats?"

Jett tucked his phone in his pocket. "We'll be right out."

"I do not need other Mannis men in the delivery room besides you, Jett."

"Technically, Will is a McCreed and I was kidding."

"You know…" She paused wiping a bead of sweat running down her cheek. "I've been thinking about baby names and seeing as we're having a boy…"

"A boy?" Jett grinned. "You've known all this time and you didn't tell me?"

"I wanted to keep it a surprise until the day. The doctor had to do an ultrasound on the visit you missed when you had the flu. There is no doubt about it being a boy from the pictures."

"You stinker." He chuckled, quickly grabbing his hat and keys from the counter before coming back to put an arm around her waist. Delia leaned on the railing, taking one slow step at a time.

"So, as I was saying," Delia continued, "I've been thinking about boy names. What would you think of naming him Reed?"

"Annie's last name? Are you sure?"

She nodded. "Do you like the idea?"

"Reed Mannis. I like it. It sounds right."

Taking her hand he led her to the passenger seat, fastening her seat belt and looking in the backseat at his son and two daughters.

*All I ever wanted.*

This was the kind of intensity he'd once numbed and now the joy he welcomed. He never wanted to miss a minute of it.

He opened the door to the backseat, taking time to lean into each child, gathering and giving kisses. Pulling himself into the driver seat, he smiled at the woman he loved.

"Okay, everybody, let's go welcome another Mannis to the family."

## Acknowledgments

Thank you to The Killion Group Inc. for an amazing cover and supporting the production of *Honeybee Rhythm*. Thank you, Barbara Bettis for expert editing and ensuring the characters and stories always stay true to the spirit of the Mercy Mountain Series.

Thank you to Laurie Cooper and Pub-Craft who partner with me to introduce readers to the resilient characters of small town Ashnee Valley through books, social media, and my website. We hope you keep coming back to visit.

To my husband and son, thank you for believing in me and my dreams.

Peace and grace to the men, women, and families in recovery support groups anywhere. Your compassion saves lives.

*Books by Becca Maxton*

**MERCY MOUNTAIN SERIES**
**Dragonfly Dance**
**Firefly Duet**

<u>Coming Next!</u>
**Cozy Christmas Crush –**
**A Mercy Mountain Novella**

For sneak peeks and the latest release dates visit *www.beccamaxton.com*

# About the Author

Becca Maxton is a contemporary romance author. She writes sensuous (dare say, steamy) and encouraging stories about rocky road detours leading to resilience and romance. Her characters are brave women and men facing challenges together and finding love.

Becca lives in Colorado with her husband and son. Follow Becca Maxton on Facebook and Instagram *@BeccaMaxtonAuthor* or visit *www.beccamaxton.com*. She enjoys meeting and connecting with readers online.

Manufactured by Amazon.ca
Acheson, AB